TOP SECRET GRAPHICA MYSTERIES

CASEBOOK: THE LOCH NESS MONSTER

Script by Justine and Ron Fontes

Layouts and Designs by Ron Fontes

Skyview Books

an imprint of
WINDMILL BOOKS
New York

Published in 2010 by Windmill Books, LLC
303 Park Avenue South, Suite # 1280
New York, NY 10010-3657

CREDITS:
Script by Justine and Ron Fontes
Layouts and designs by Ron Fontes
Art by Planman, Ltd.

Publisher Cataloging in Publication

Fontes, Justine
        Casebook--the Loch Ness monster. – School and library ed. / script by Justine
and Ron Fontes; layouts and designs by Ron Fontes; art by Planman, Ltd.
p.   cm. – (Top secret graphica mysteries)
Summary: Einstein and his friends use their virtual visors to investigate the
origins of Loch Ness, stories about the monster first reported to live there in 565 A.D.,
eyewitness reports, and possible explanations.
ISBN 978-1-60754-602-3. – ISBN 978-1-60754-600-9 (pbk.)
ISBN 978-1-60754-601-6 (6-pack)
        1. Loch Ness monster—Juvenile fiction   2. Graphic novels   [1. Loch
Ness monster—Fiction   2. Monsters—Fiction   3. Graphic novels]   I. Fontes, Ron
II. Title   III. Title: Loch Ness monster   IV. Series
        741.5/973—dc22

Manufactured in the United States of America

CONTENTS

Welcome to the Windmill Bakery

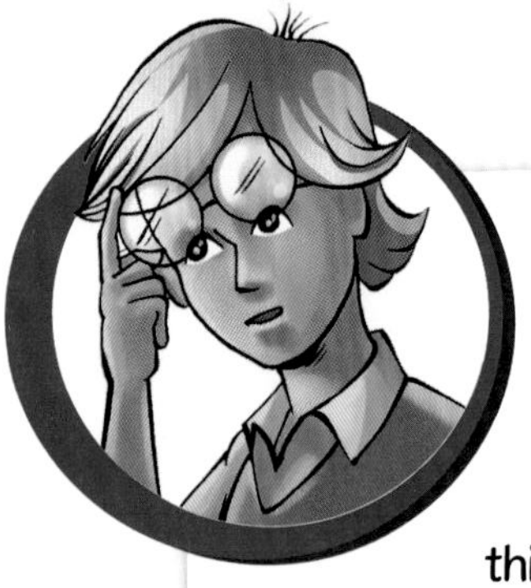

Edward Icarus Stein is known as "Einstein" because of his initials "E.I." and his last name, and because he loves science the way fanatical fans love sports. Einstein dedicates his waking hours to observing as much as he can of all the strange things just beyond human knowledge, because "that's the discovery zone," as he calls it. Einstein aspires to nothing less than living up to his nickname and coming up with a truly groundbreaking scientific discovery. So far this brilliant seventh grader's best invention is the Virtual Visors he and his friends use to explore strange phenomena. Einstein's parents own the local bakery where the friends meet.

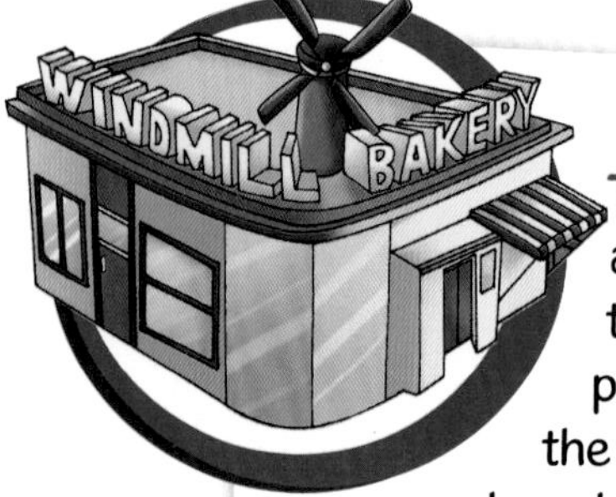
WINDMILL BAKERY

The Windmill Bakery is a cozy place where friends and neighbors buy homemade goodies to go or to eat on the premises. Einstein's kindhearted parents make everyone feel welcome, especially the friends who understand their exceptional son and share his appetite for discovery!

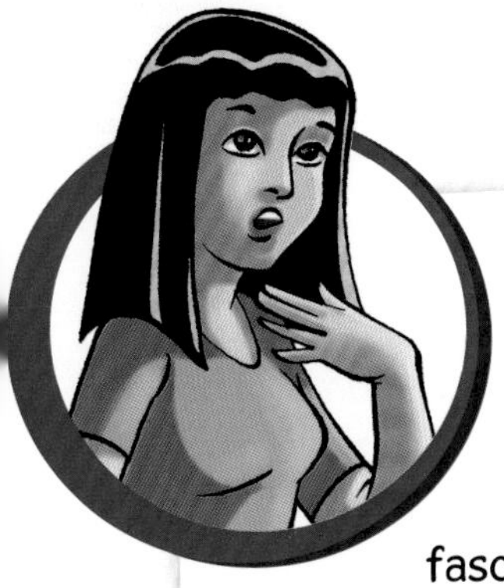

"Spacey Tracy" Lee saw a UFO when she was seven. Her parents tried to dismiss the incident as a "waking dream." But Tracy knew what she saw and it inspired her to investigate the UFO phenomenon. The more she learned, the more fascinated she became. She earned her nickname by constantly talking about UFOs. Tracy hopes to become a reporter when she grows up so she can continue to explore the unknown. A straight-A student, Tracy enjoys swimming, gymnastics, and playing the cello. Now that she's "more mature" and hoping to lose the silly nickname, Tracy shares the experience that changed her life forever only with her Virtual Visor buddies.

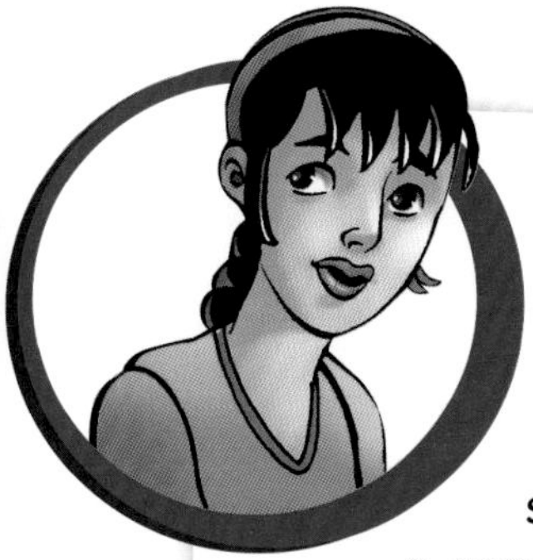

Clarita Gonzales knows that Indiana Jones and Lara Croft aren't real people, but that doesn't stop this seventh grader from wanting to be an adventurous archaeologist. Clarita's parents will support any path she chooses, as long as she gets a good education. Unfortunately, school isn't her strong point. During most classes, Clarita's mind wanders to, as she puts it, "more exciting places—like Atlantis!" A tomboy thanks to her three older brothers and one younger brother, Clarita is a great soccer player and is also into martial arts. Her interest in archaeology extends to architecture, artifacts, cooking, and all forms of culture. (Clarita would have a crush on Einstein if he wasn't "such a bookworm")!

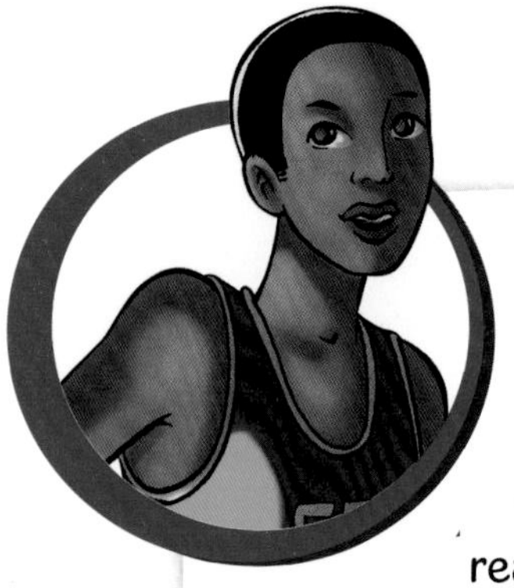

"Freaky Frank" Phillips earned his nickname because of his uncanny ability to use his "extra senses," a "gift" he inherited from his grandma. Though this eighth grader can't predict the winners of the next SUPERBOWL (or, he admits, "anything really useful"), Frank "knows" when someone is lying or otherwise up to no good. He gets "warnings" before trouble strikes. And sometimes he "sees things that aren't there"—at least to those less sensitive to things like auras and ghosts. Frank isn't sure what he wants to be when he grows up. He enjoys keeping tropical fish and does well in every subject, except math. "Numbers make my head hurt," Frank confesses. Frank spends lots of time with his family and his fish, but he's always up for an adventure with his friends.

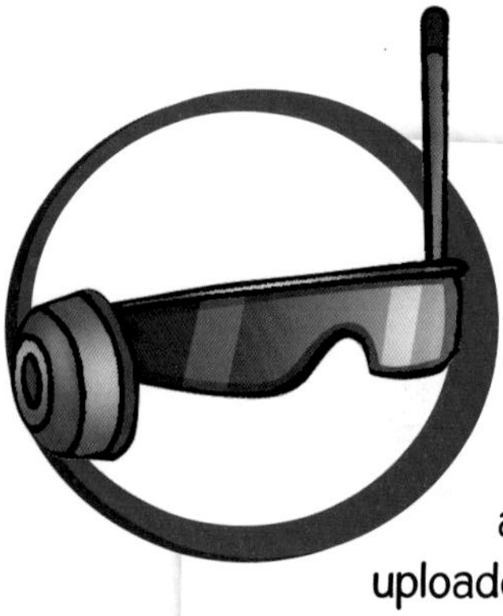

The Virtual Visors allow Einstein, Frank, Clarita, and Tracy to pursue their taste for adventure well beyond the boundaries of the bakery. Thanks to Einstein's brilliant software, the visors can simulate all kinds of locations and experiences based on the uploaded facts. Once inside the program, the visors become invisible. When danger gets too intense, the kids can always touch their Virtual Visors to return to the bakery. Sometimes the kids explore in the real world without the visors. But more often they use these devices to explore the mysteries and phenomena that intrigue each member of the group. The Virtual Visors are the ultimate virtual reality research tool, even though you never know what quirky things might happen thanks to Einstein's "Random Adventure Program."

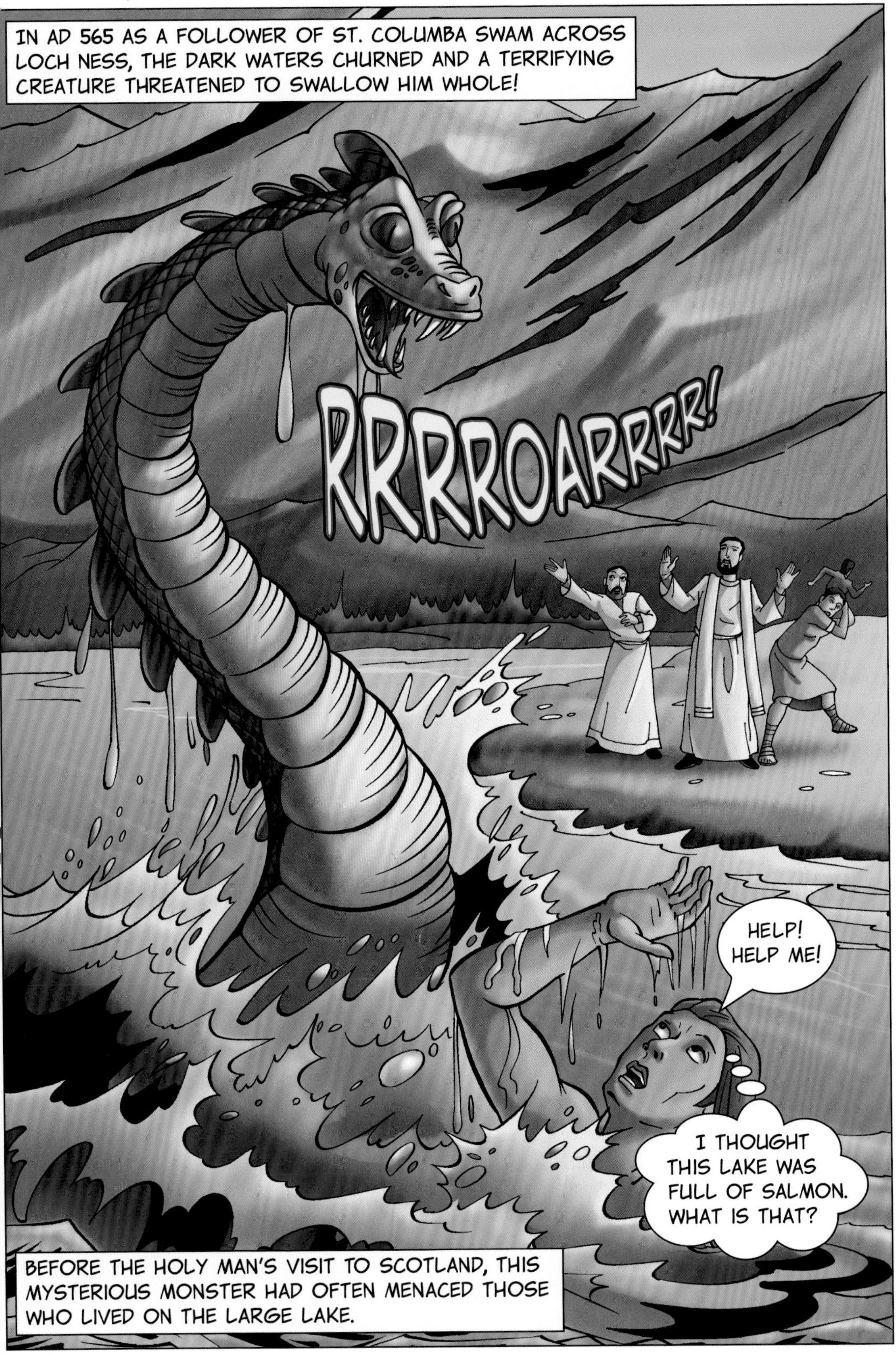
IN AD 565 AS A FOLLOWER OF ST. COLUMBA SWAM ACROSS LOCH NESS, THE DARK WATERS CHURNED AND A TERRIFYING CREATURE THREATENED TO SWALLOW HIM WHOLE!
RRRROARRRR!
HELP! HELP ME!
I THOUGHT THIS LAKE WAS FULL OF SALMON. WHAT IS THAT?
BEFORE THE HOLY MAN'S VISIT TO SCOTLAND, THIS MYSTERIOUS MONSTER HAD OFTEN MENACED THOSE WHO LIVED ON THE LARGE LAKE.

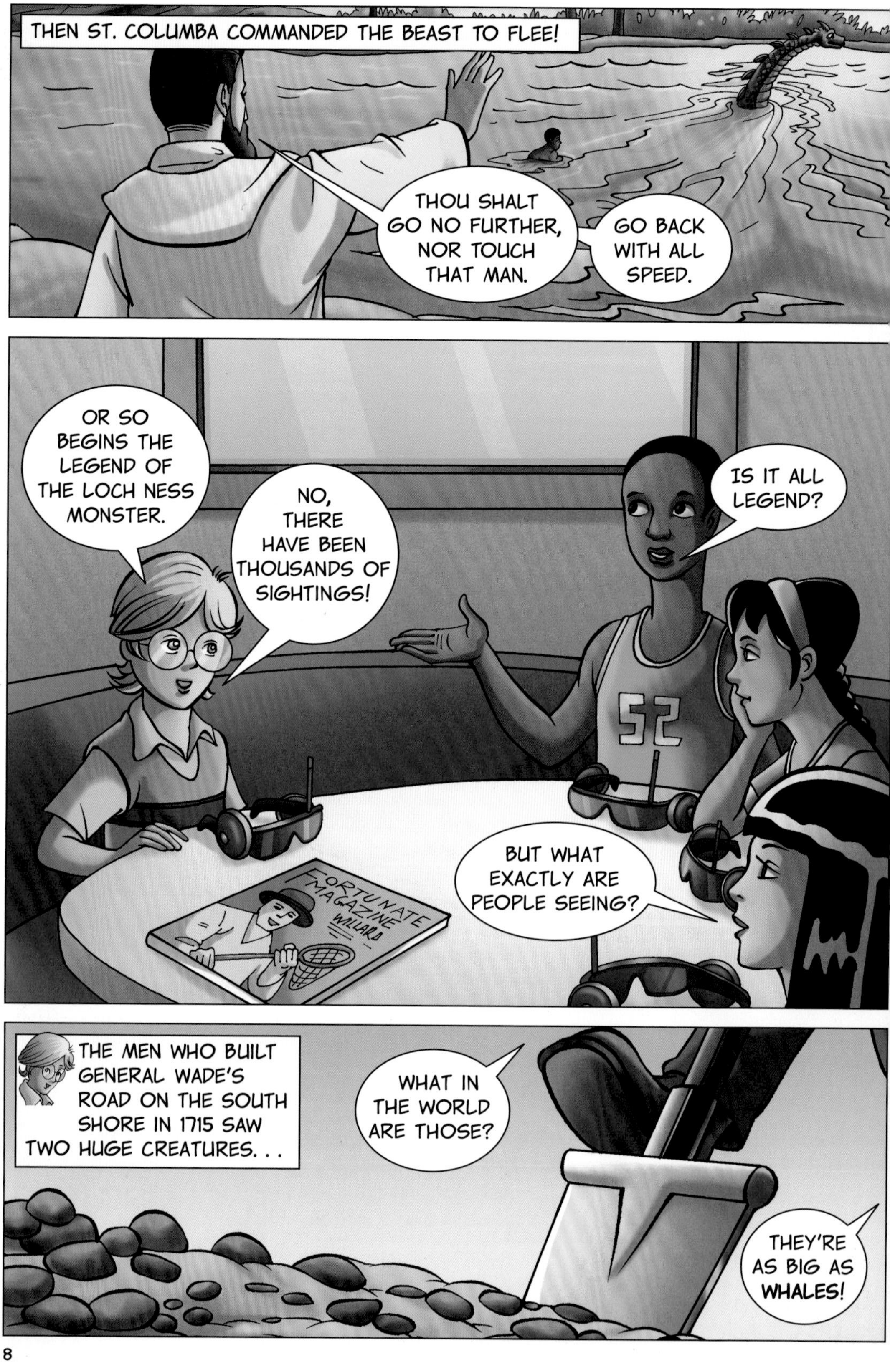
THEN ST. COLUMBA COMMANDED THE BEAST TO FLEE!
THOU SHALT GO NO FURTHER, NOR TOUCH THAT MAN.
GO BACK WITH ALL SPEED.
OR SO BEGINS THE LEGEND OF THE LOCH NESS MONSTER.
IS IT ALL LEGEND?
NO, THERE HAVE BEEN THOUSANDS OF SIGHTINGS!
BUT WHAT EXACTLY ARE PEOPLE SEEING?
FORTUNATE MAGAZINE
WILLARD
THE MEN WHO BUILT GENERAL WADE'S ROAD ON THE SOUTH SHORE IN 1715 SAW TWO HUGE CREATURES. . .
WHAT IN THE WORLD ARE THOSE?
THEY'RE AS BIG AS WHALES!

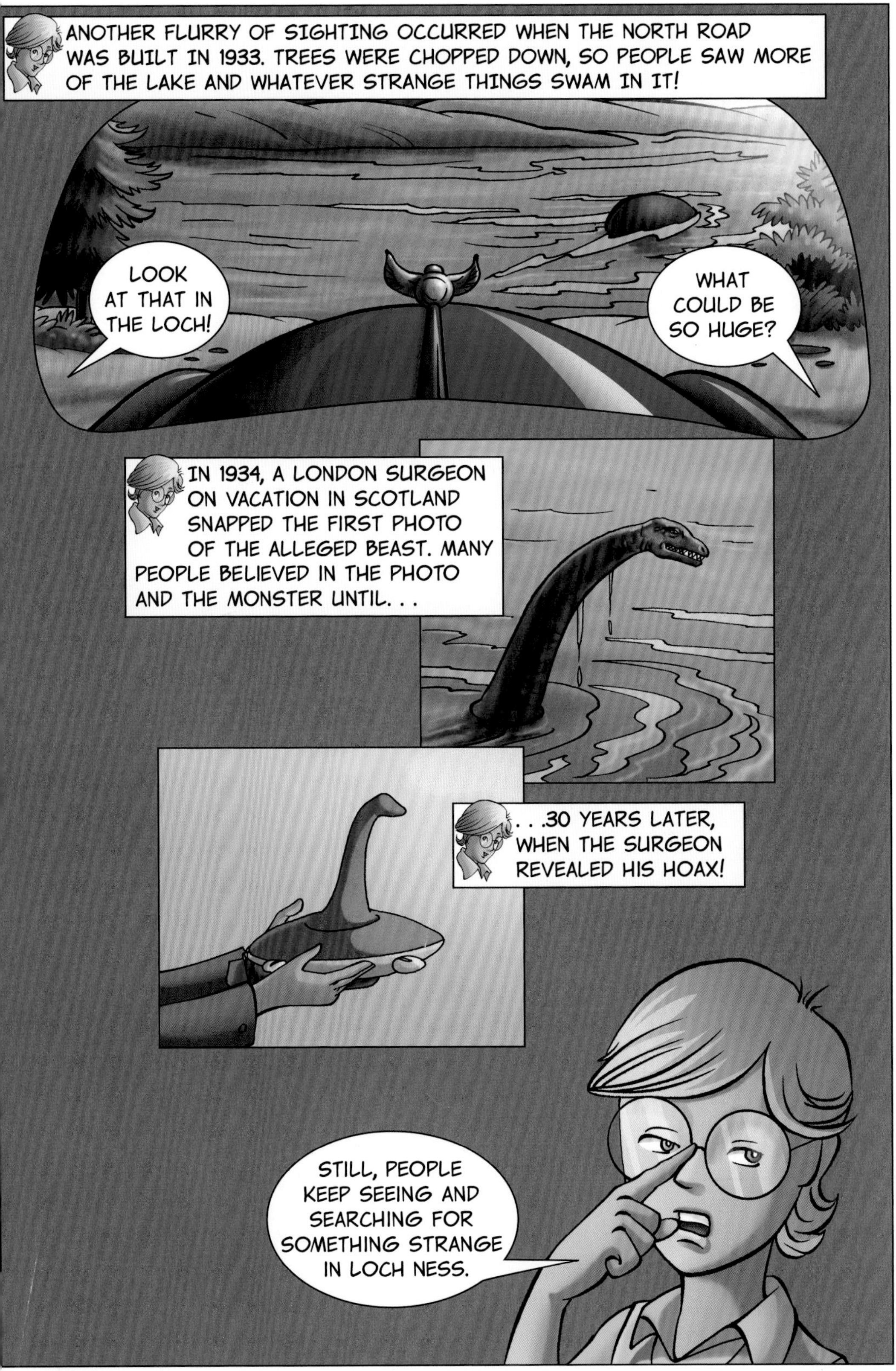
ANOTHER FLURRY OF SIGHTING OCCURRED WHEN THE NORTH ROAD WAS BUILT IN 1933. TREES WERE CHOPPED DOWN, SO PEOPLE SAW MORE OF THE LAKE AND WHATEVER STRANGE THINGS SWAM IN IT!
LOOK AT THAT IN THE LOCH!
WHAT COULD BE SO HUGE?
IN 1934, A LONDON SURGEON ON VACATION IN SCOTLAND SNAPPED THE FIRST PHOTO OF THE ALLEGED BEAST. MANY PEOPLE BELIEVED IN THE PHOTO AND THE MONSTER UNTIL. . .
. . .30 YEARS LATER, WHEN THE SURGEON REVEALED HIS HOAX!
STILL, PEOPLE KEEP SEEING AND SEARCHING FOR SOMETHING STRANGE IN LOCH NESS.

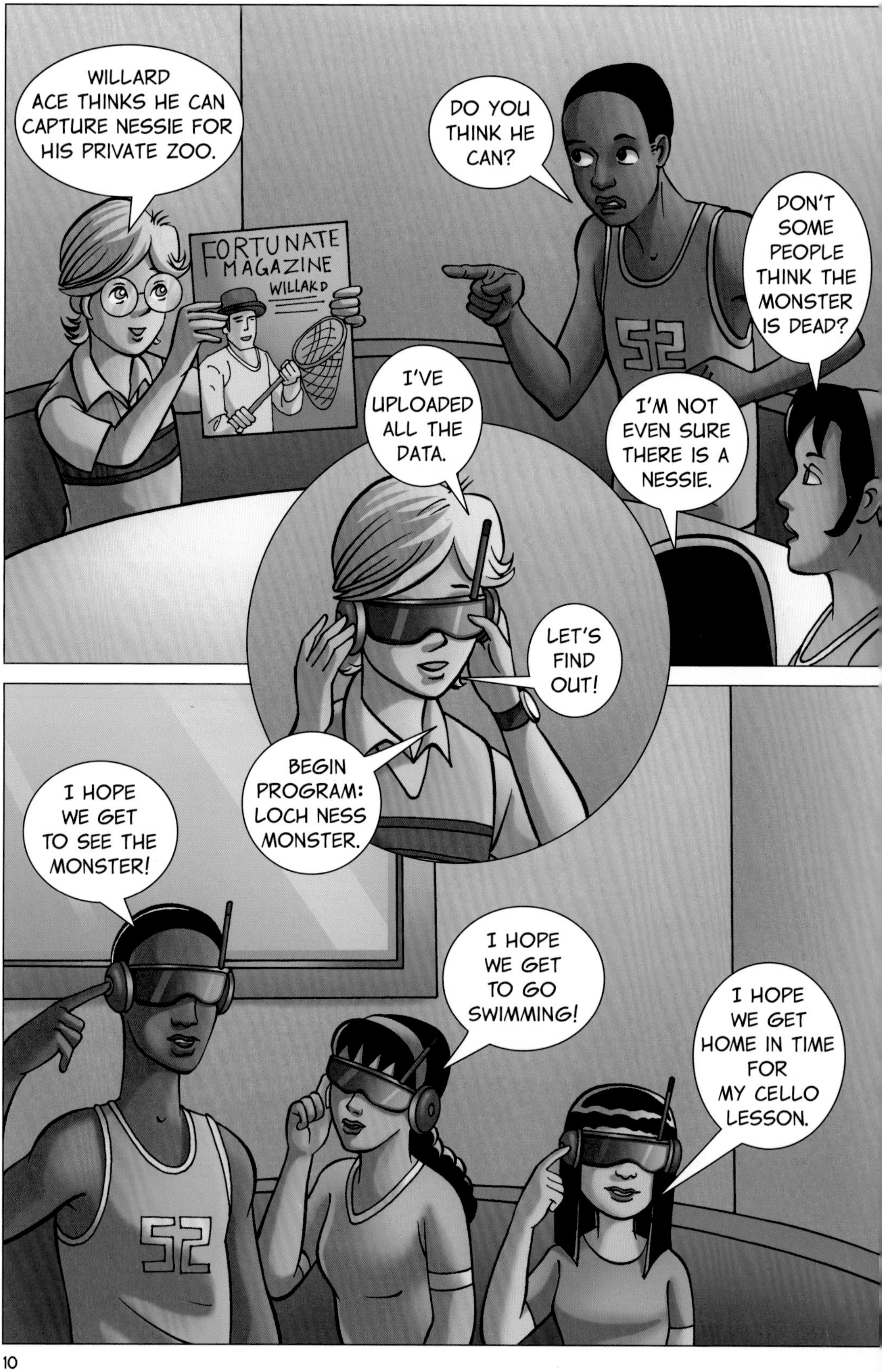
WILLARD ACE THINKS HE CAN CAPTURE NESSIE FOR HIS PRIVATE ZOO.
FORTUNATE MAGAZINE
WILLARD
DO YOU THINK HE CAN?
DON'T SOME PEOPLE THINK THE MONSTER IS DEAD?
I'M NOT EVEN SURE THERE IS A NESSIE.
I'VE UPLOADED ALL THE DATA.
LET'S FIND OUT!
BEGIN PROGRAM: LOCH NESS MONSTER.
I HOPE WE GET TO SEE THE MONSTER!
I HOPE WE GET TO GO SWIMMING!
I HOPE WE GET HOME IN TIME FOR MY CELLO LESSON.

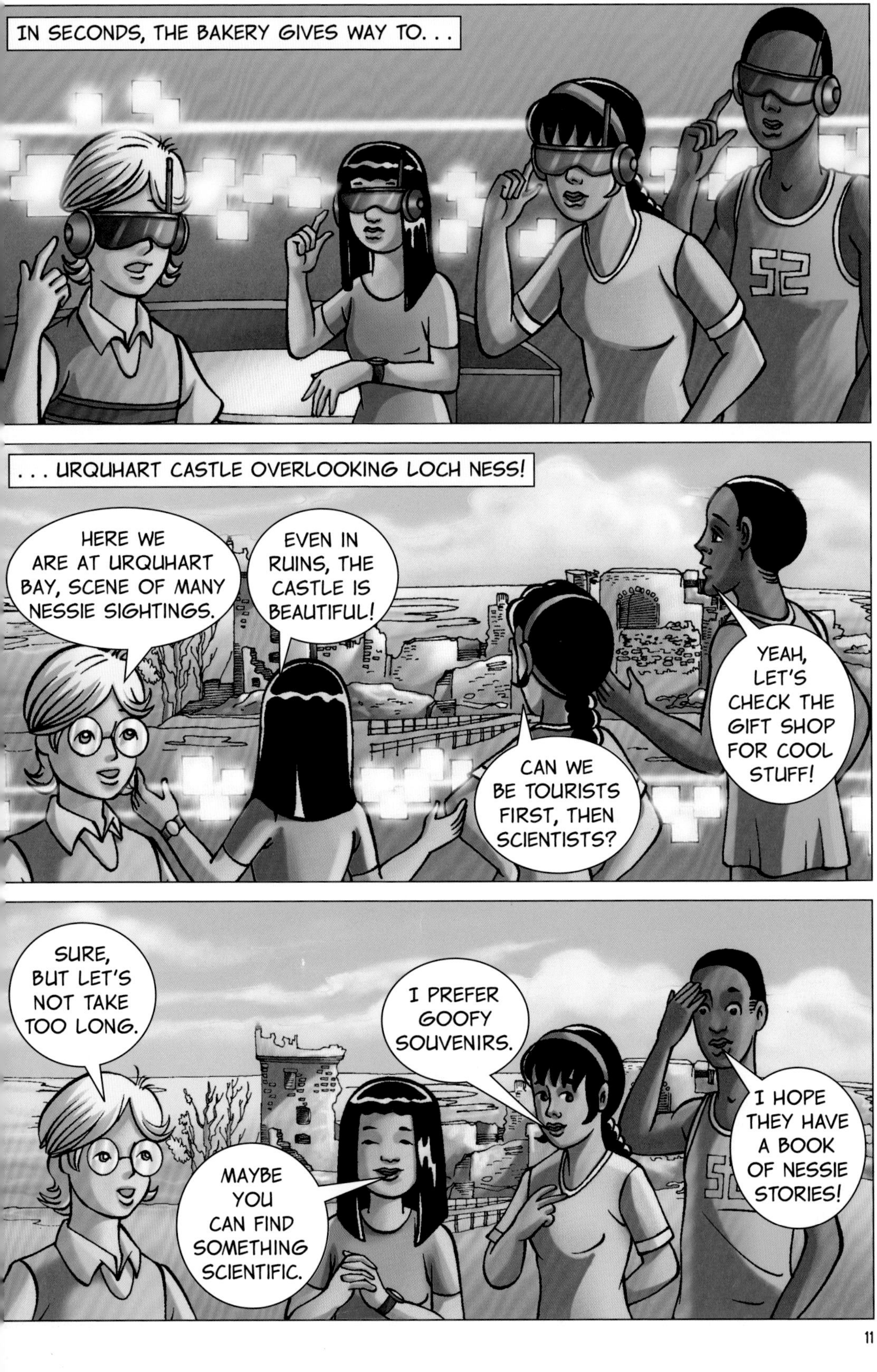
IN SECONDS, THE BAKERY GIVES WAY TO. . .
. . . URQUHART CASTLE OVERLOOKING LOCH NESS!
HERE WE ARE AT URQUHART BAY, SCENE OF MANY NESSIE SIGHTINGS.
EVEN IN RUINS, THE CASTLE IS BEAUTIFUL!
CAN WE BE TOURISTS FIRST, THEN SCIENTISTS?
YEAH, LET'S CHECK THE GIFT SHOP FOR COOL STUFF!
SURE, BUT LET'S NOT TAKE TOO LONG.
MAYBE YOU CAN FIND SOMETHING SCIENTIFIC.
I PREFER GOOFY SOUVENIRS.
I HOPE THEY HAVE A BOOK OF NESSIE STORIES!

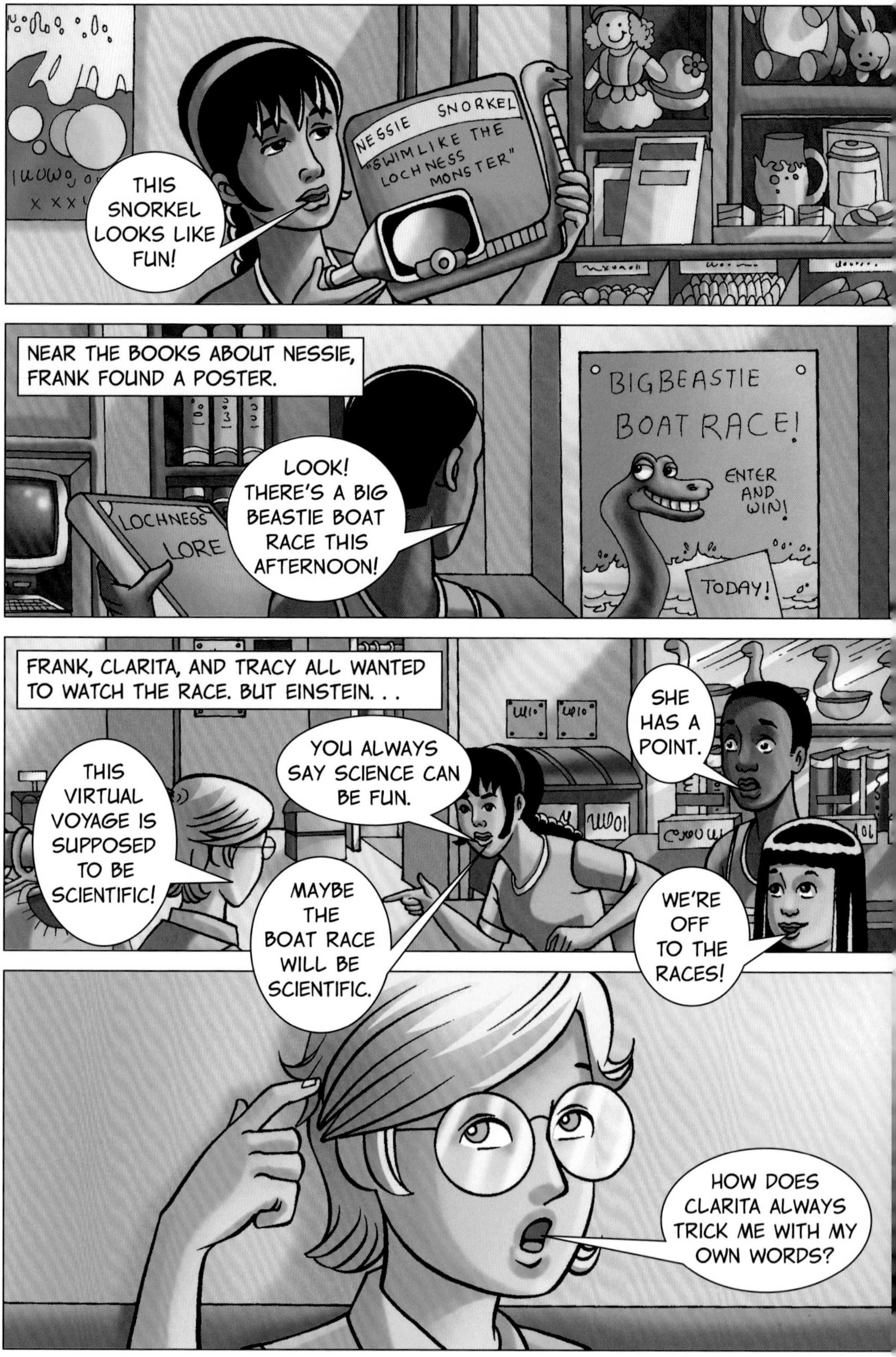
THIS SNORKEL LOOKS LIKE FUN!
NESSIE SNORKEL "SWIM LIKE THE LOCHNESS MONSTER"
NEAR THE BOOKS ABOUT NESSIE, FRANK FOUND A POSTER.
LOOK! THERE'S A BIG BEASTIE BOAT RACE THIS AFTERNOON!
LOCHNESS LORE
BIGBEASTIE BOAT RACE!
ENTER AND WIN!
TODAY!
FRANK, CLARITA, AND TRACY ALL WANTED TO WATCH THE RACE. BUT EINSTEIN. . .
THIS VIRTUAL VOYAGE IS SUPPOSED TO BE SCIENTIFIC!
YOU ALWAYS SAY SCIENCE CAN BE FUN.
MAYBE THE BOAT RACE WILL BE SCIENTIFIC.
SHE HAS A POINT.
WE'RE OFF TO THE RACES!
HOW DOES CLARITA ALWAYS TRICK ME WITH MY OWN WORDS?

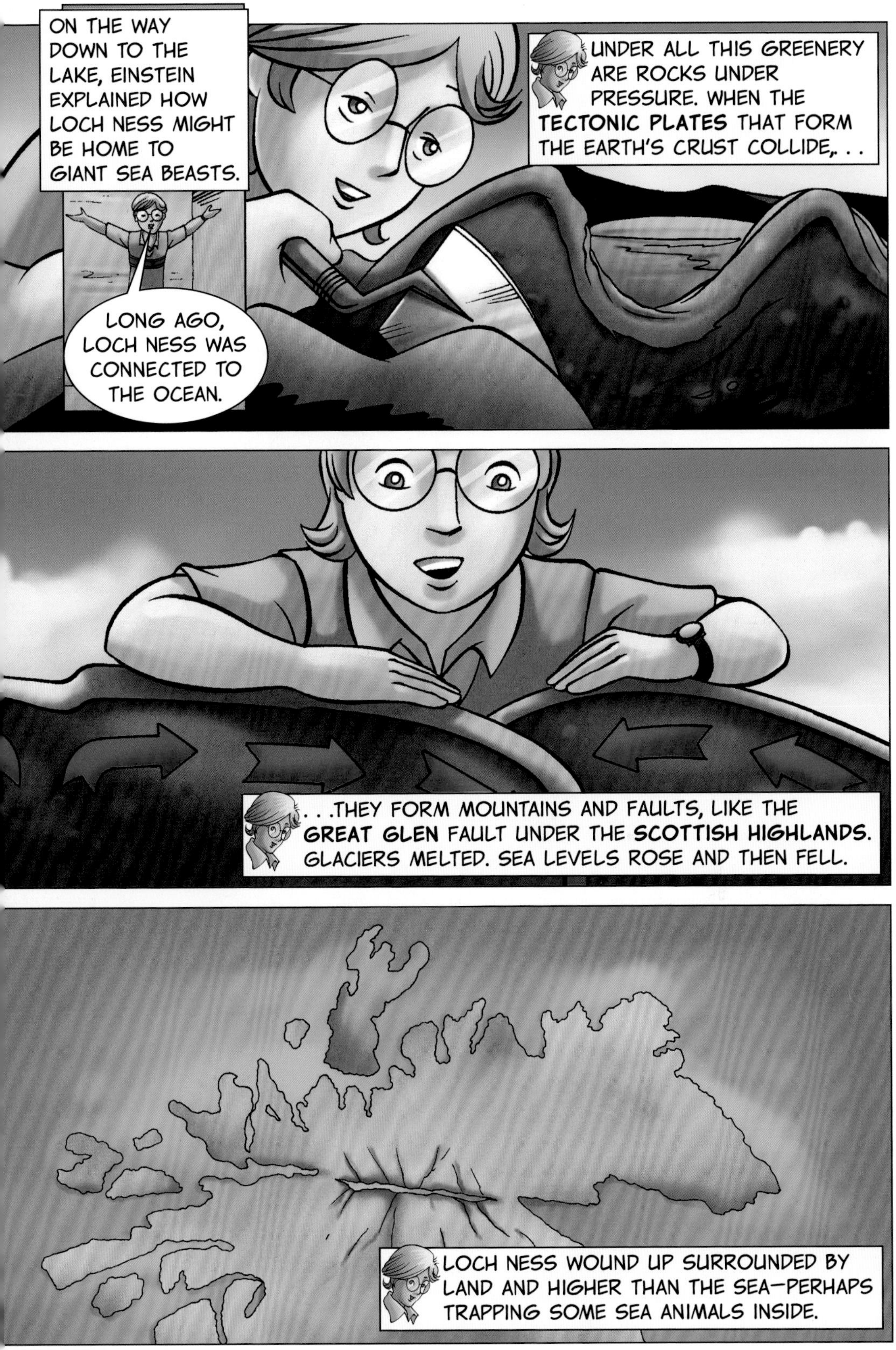
ON THE WAY DOWN TO THE LAKE, EINSTEIN EXPLAINED HOW LOCH NESS MIGHT BE HOME TO GIANT SEA BEASTS.
LONG AGO, LOCH NESS WAS CONNECTED TO THE OCEAN.
UNDER ALL THIS GREENERY ARE ROCKS UNDER PRESSURE. WHEN THE **TECTONIC PLATES** THAT FORM THE EARTH'S CRUST COLLIDE,. . .
. . .THEY FORM MOUNTAINS AND FAULTS, LIKE THE **GREAT GLEN** FAULT UNDER THE **SCOTTISH HIGHLANDS**. GLACIERS MELTED. SEA LEVELS ROSE AND THEN FELL.
LOCH NESS WOUND UP SURROUNDED BY LAND AND HIGHER THAN THE SEA—PERHAPS TRAPPING SOME SEA ANIMALS INSIDE.

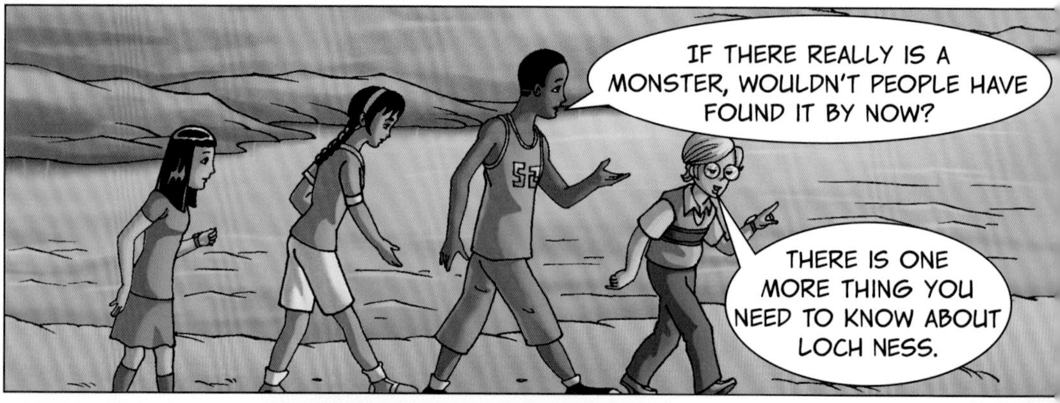
IF THERE REALLY IS A MONSTER, WOULDN'T PEOPLE HAVE FOUND IT BY NOW?
THERE IS ONE MORE THING YOU NEED TO KNOW ABOUT LOCH NESS.

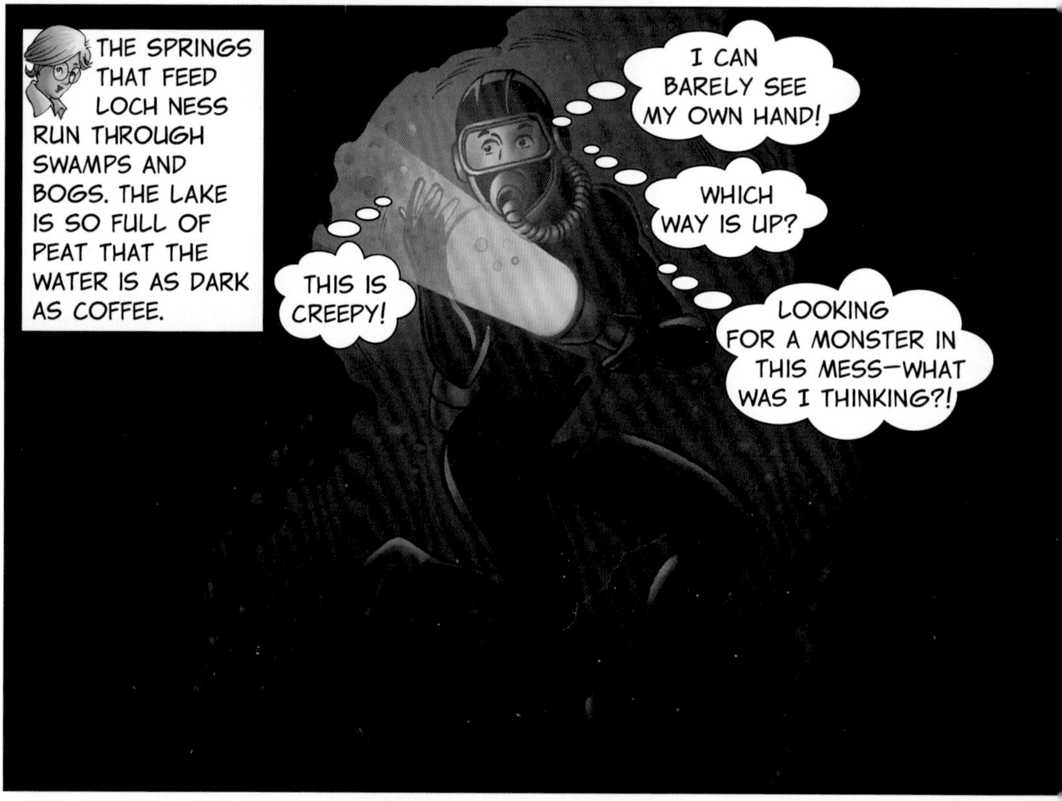
THE SPRINGS THAT FEED LOCH NESS RUN THROUGH SWAMPS AND BOGS. THE LAKE IS SO FULL OF PEAT THAT THE WATER IS AS DARK AS COFFEE.
I CAN BARELY SEE MY OWN HAND!
WHICH WAY IS UP?
THIS IS CREEPY!
LOOKING FOR A MONSTER IN THIS MESS—WHAT WAS I THINKING?!

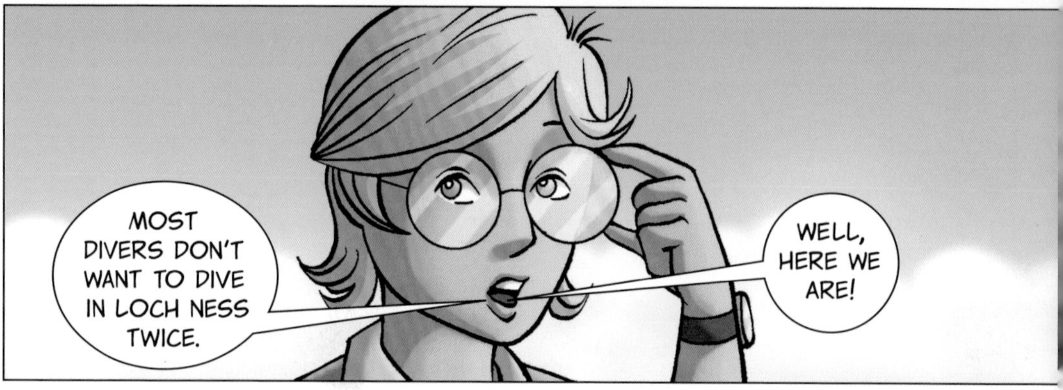
MOST DIVERS DON'T WANT TO DIVE IN LOCH NESS TWICE.
WELL, HERE WE ARE!

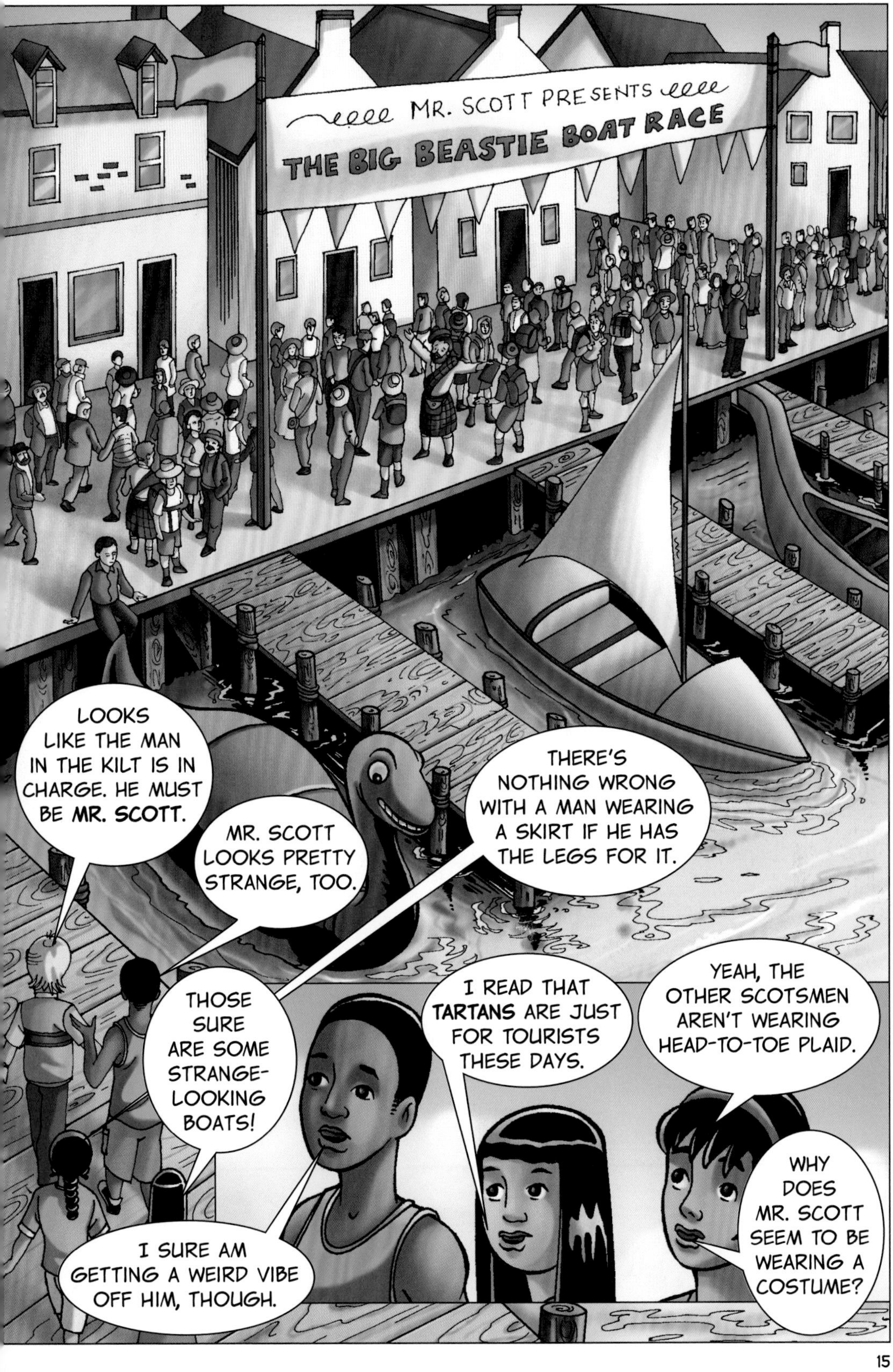
MR. SCOTT PRESENTS
THE BIG BEASTIE BOAT RACE
LOOKS LIKE THE MAN IN THE KILT IS IN CHARGE. HE MUST BE **MR. SCOTT**.
MR. SCOTT LOOKS PRETTY STRANGE, TOO.
THERE'S NOTHING WRONG WITH A MAN WEARING A SKIRT IF HE HAS THE LEGS FOR IT.
THOSE SURE ARE SOME STRANGE-LOOKING BOATS!
I SURE AM GETTING A WEIRD VIBE OFF HIM, THOUGH.
I READ THAT **TARTANS** ARE JUST FOR TOURISTS THESE DAYS.
YEAH, THE OTHER SCOTSMEN AREN'T WEARING HEAD-TO-TOE PLAID.
WHY DOES MR. SCOTT SEEM TO BE WEARING A COSTUME?

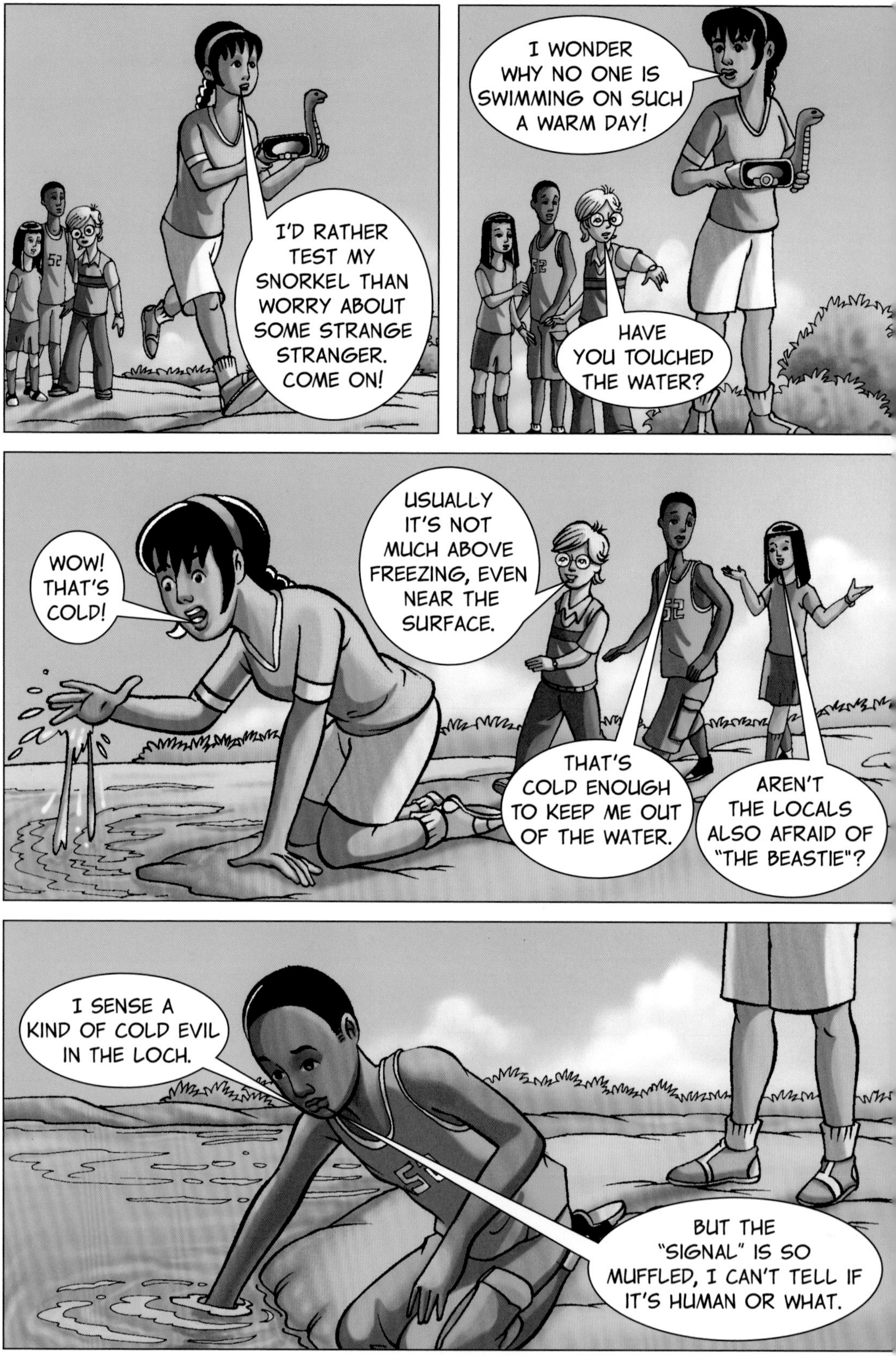
I'D RATHER TEST MY SNORKEL THAN WORRY ABOUT SOME STRANGE STRANGER. COME ON!
I WONDER WHY NO ONE IS SWIMMING ON SUCH A WARM DAY!
HAVE YOU TOUCHED THE WATER?
WOW! THAT'S COLD!
USUALLY IT'S NOT MUCH ABOVE FREEZING, EVEN NEAR THE SURFACE.
THAT'S COLD ENOUGH TO KEEP ME OUT OF THE WATER.
AREN'T THE LOCALS ALSO AFRAID OF "THE BEASTIE"?
I SENSE A KIND OF COLD EVIL IN THE LOCH.
BUT THE "SIGNAL" IS SO MUFFLED, I CAN'T TELL IF IT'S HUMAN OR WHAT.

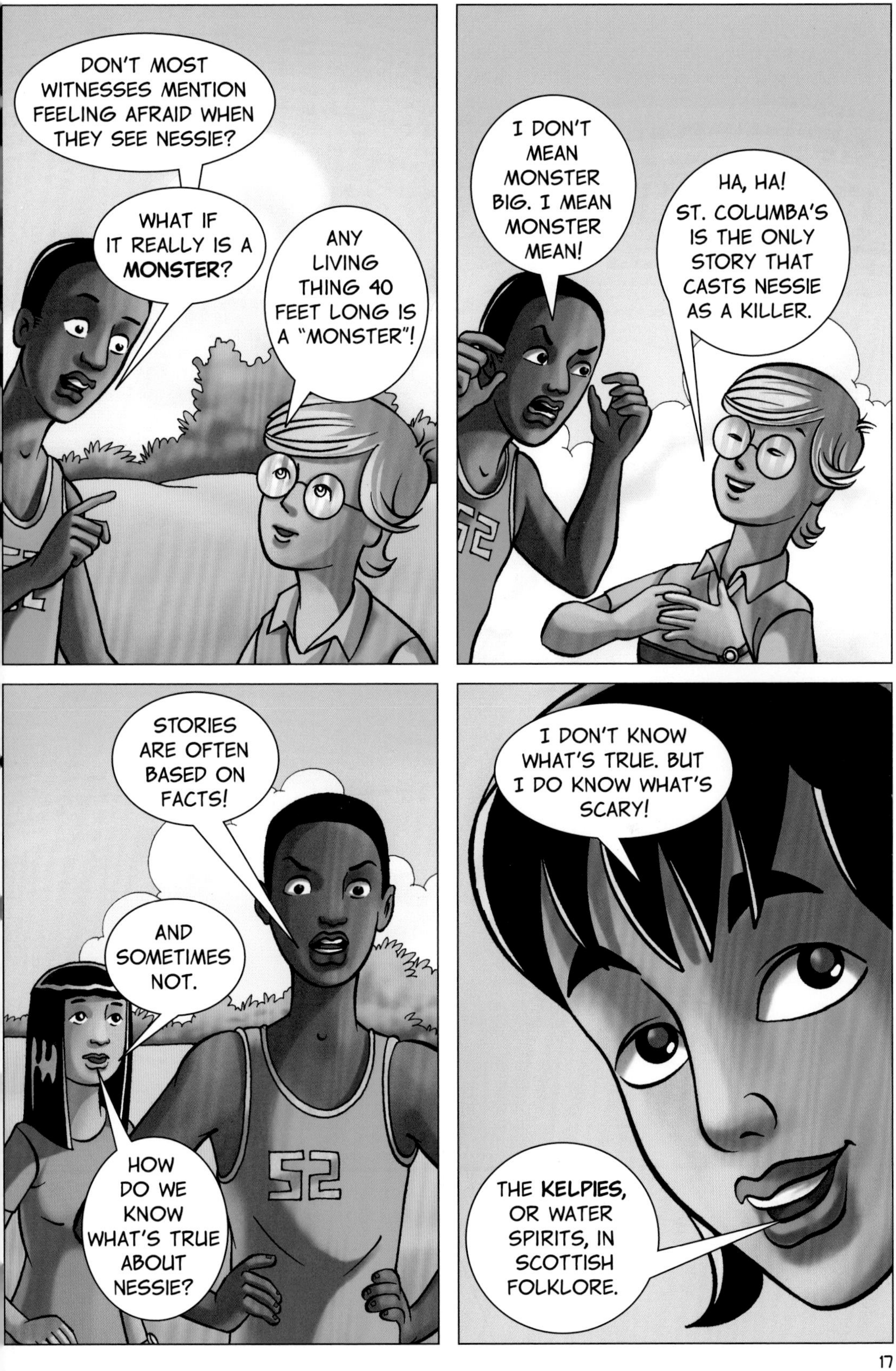
DON'T MOST WITNESSES MENTION FEELING AFRAID WHEN THEY SEE NESSIE?
WHAT IF IT REALLY IS A **MONSTER**?
ANY LIVING THING 40 FEET LONG IS A "MONSTER"!
I DON'T MEAN MONSTER BIG. I MEAN MONSTER MEAN!
HA, HA! ST. COLUMBA'S IS THE ONLY STORY THAT CASTS NESSIE AS A KILLER.
STORIES ARE OFTEN BASED ON FACTS!
AND SOMETIMES NOT.
HOW DO WE KNOW WHAT'S TRUE ABOUT NESSIE?
I DON'T KNOW WHAT'S TRUE. BUT I DO KNOW WHAT'S SCARY!
THE **KELPIES,** OR WATER SPIRITS, IN SCOTTISH FOLKLORE.

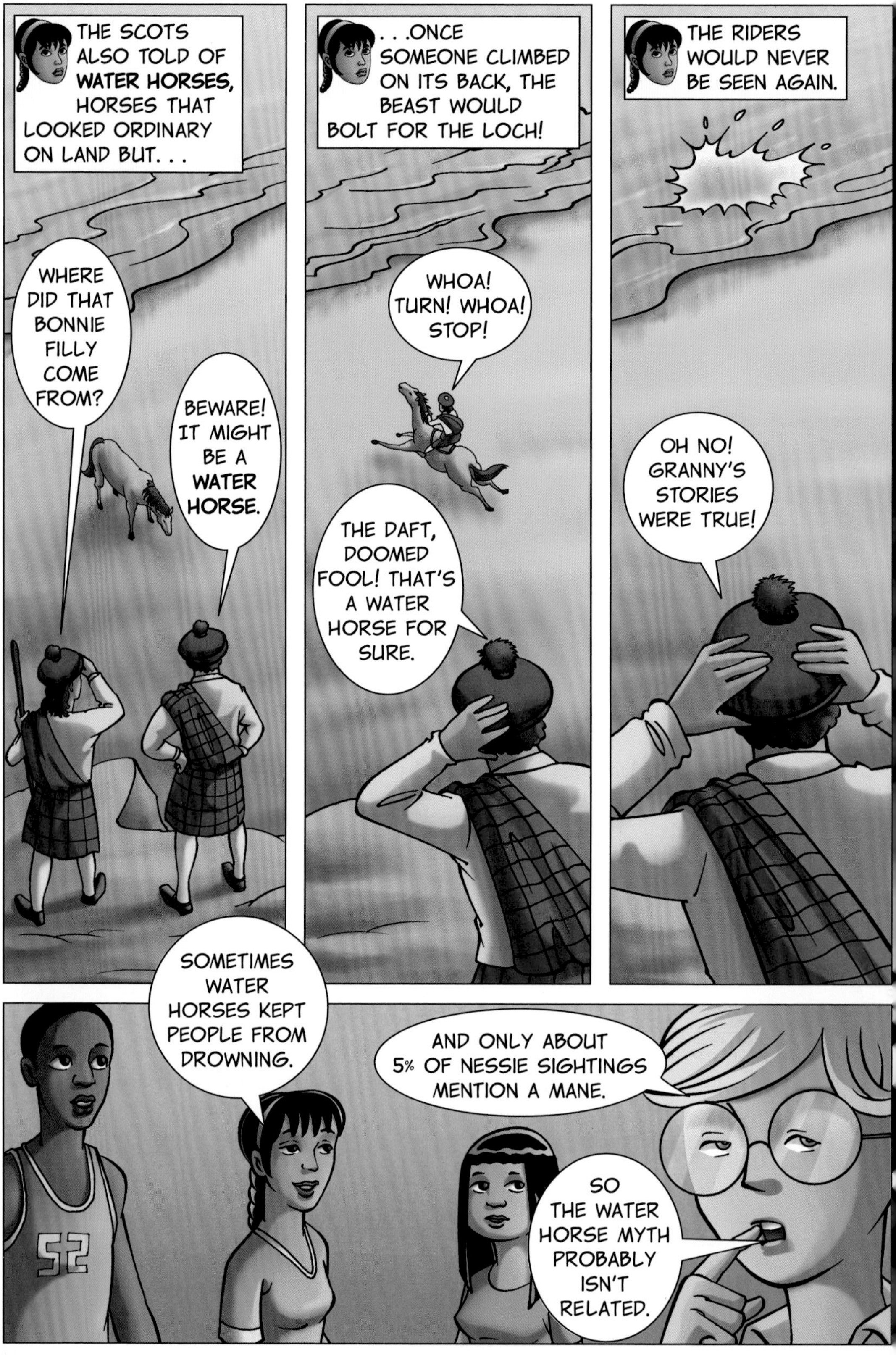
THE SCOTS ALSO TOLD OF **WATER HORSES,** HORSES THAT LOOKED ORDINARY ON LAND BUT. . .
WHERE DID THAT BONNIE FILLY COME FROM?
BEWARE! IT MIGHT BE A **WATER HORSE.**
. . .ONCE SOMEONE CLIMBED ON ITS BACK, THE BEAST WOULD BOLT FOR THE LOCH!
WHOA! TURN! WHOA! STOP!
THE DAFT, DOOMED FOOL! THAT'S A WATER HORSE FOR SURE.
THE RIDERS WOULD NEVER BE SEEN AGAIN.
OH NO! GRANNY'S STORIES WERE TRUE!
SOMETIMES WATER HORSES KEPT PEOPLE FROM DROWNING.
AND ONLY ABOUT 5% OF NESSIE SIGHTINGS MENTION A MANE.
SO THE WATER HORSE MYTH PROBABLY ISN'T RELATED.
52

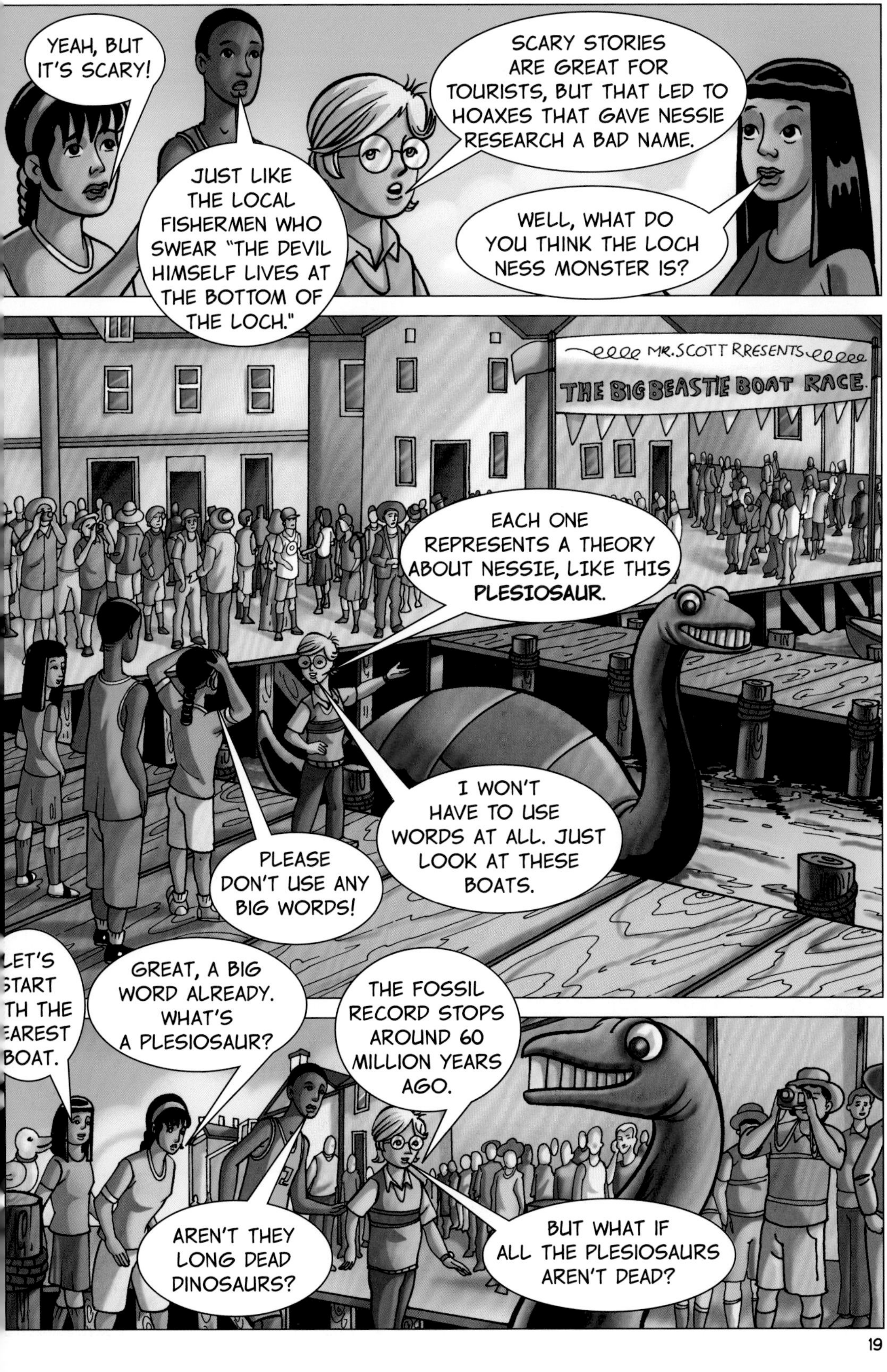
YEAH, BUT IT'S SCARY!
JUST LIKE THE LOCAL FISHERMEN WHO SWEAR "THE DEVIL HIMSELF LIVES AT THE BOTTOM OF THE LOCH."
SCARY STORIES ARE GREAT FOR TOURISTS, BUT THAT LED TO HOAXES THAT GAVE NESSIE RESEARCH A BAD NAME.
WELL, WHAT DO YOU THINK THE LOCH NESS MONSTER IS?
MR. SCOTT RRESENTS
THE BIG BEASTIE BOAT RACE
EACH ONE REPRESENTS A THEORY ABOUT NESSIE, LIKE THIS **PLESIOSAUR**.
PLEASE DON'T USE ANY BIG WORDS!
I WON'T HAVE TO USE WORDS AT ALL. JUST LOOK AT THESE BOATS.
LET'S START TH THE EAREST BOAT.
GREAT, A BIG WORD ALREADY. WHAT'S A PLESIOSAUR?
THE FOSSIL RECORD STOPS AROUND 60 MILLION YEARS AGO.
AREN'T THEY LONG DEAD DINOSAURS?
BUT WHAT IF ALL THE PLESIOSAURS AREN'T DEAD?

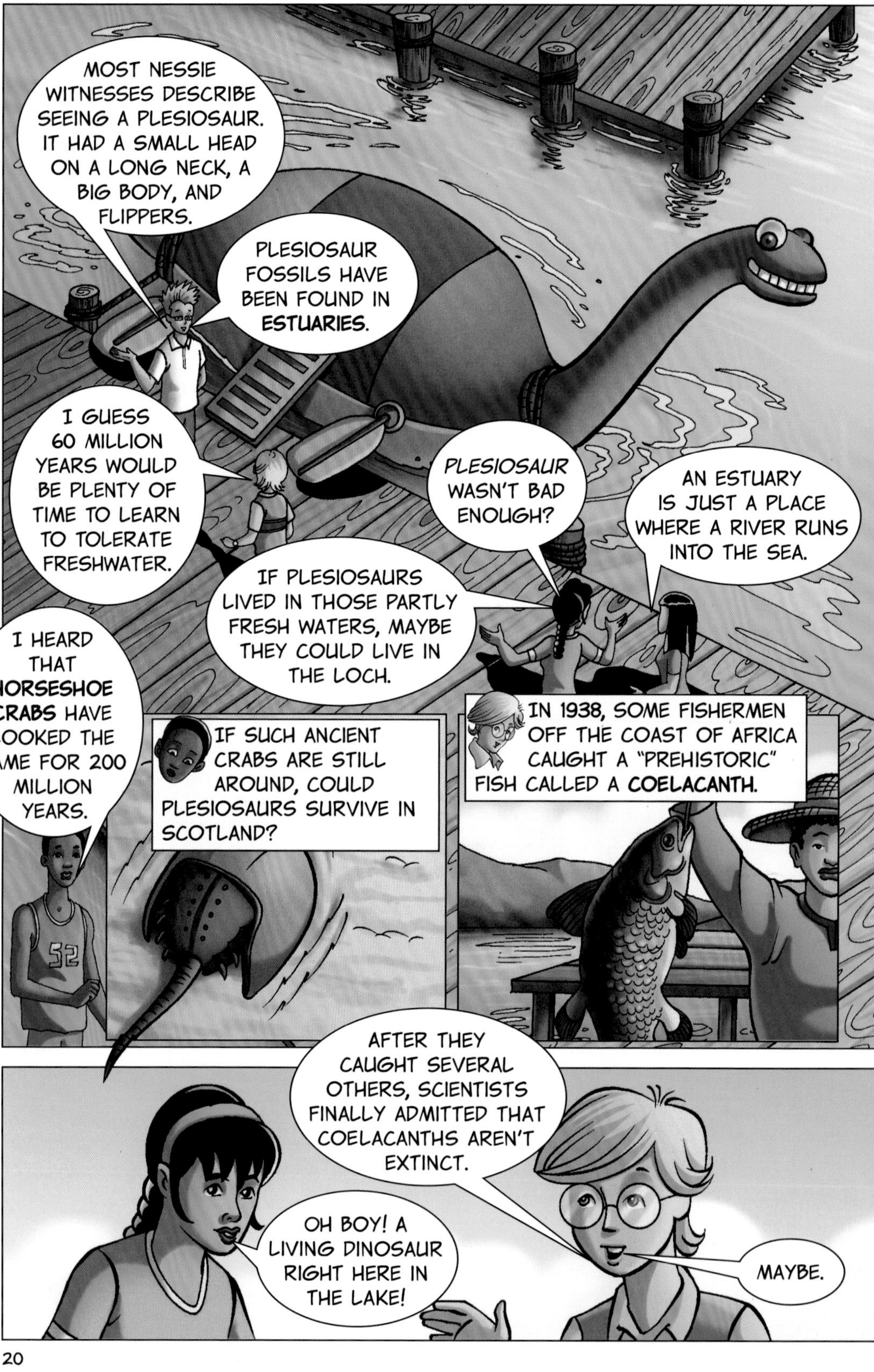
MOST NESSIE WITNESSES DESCRIBE SEEING A PLESIOSAUR. IT HAD A SMALL HEAD ON A LONG NECK, A BIG BODY, AND FLIPPERS.
PLESIOSAUR FOSSILS HAVE BEEN FOUND IN **ESTUARIES**.
I GUESS 60 MILLION YEARS WOULD BE PLENTY OF TIME TO LEARN TO TOLERATE FRESHWATER.
PLESIOSAUR WASN'T BAD ENOUGH?
AN ESTUARY IS JUST A PLACE WHERE A RIVER RUNS INTO THE SEA.
IF PLESIOSAURS LIVED IN THOSE PARTLY FRESH WATERS, MAYBE THEY COULD LIVE IN THE LOCH.
I HEARD THAT **HORSESHOE CRABS** HAVE LOOKED THE SAME FOR 200 MILLION YEARS.
IF SUCH ANCIENT CRABS ARE STILL AROUND, COULD PLESIOSAURS SURVIVE IN SCOTLAND?
IN 1938, SOME FISHERMEN OFF THE COAST OF AFRICA CAUGHT A "PREHISTORIC" FISH CALLED A **COELACANTH**.
AFTER THEY CAUGHT SEVERAL OTHERS, SCIENTISTS FINALLY ADMITTED THAT COELACANTHS AREN'T EXTINCT.
OH BOY! A LIVING DINOSAUR RIGHT HERE IN THE LAKE!
MAYBE.

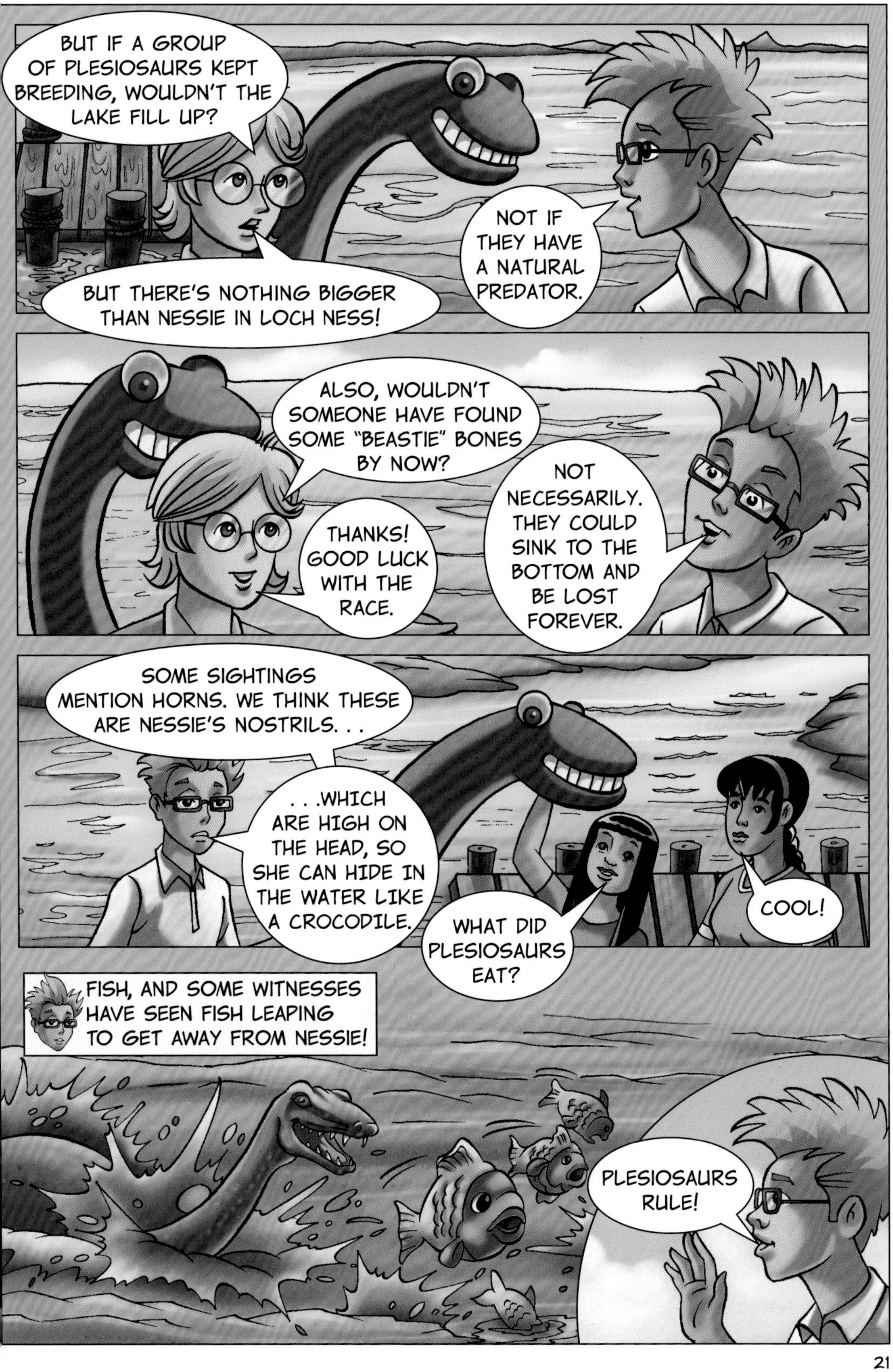
BUT IF A GROUP OF PLESIOSAURS KEPT BREEDING, WOULDN'T THE LAKE FILL UP?
NOT IF THEY HAVE A NATURAL PREDATOR.
BUT THERE'S NOTHING BIGGER THAN NESSIE IN LOCH NESS!
ALSO, WOULDN'T SOMEONE HAVE FOUND SOME "BEASTIE" BONES BY NOW?
NOT NECESSARILY. THEY COULD SINK TO THE BOTTOM AND BE LOST FOREVER.
THANKS! GOOD LUCK WITH THE RACE.
SOME SIGHTINGS MENTION HORNS. WE THINK THESE ARE NESSIE'S NOSTRILS. . .
. . .WHICH ARE HIGH ON THE HEAD, SO SHE CAN HIDE IN THE WATER LIKE A CROCODILE.
WHAT DID PLESIOSAURS EAT?
COOL!
FISH, AND SOME WITNESSES HAVE SEEN FISH LEAPING TO GET AWAY FROM NESSIE!
PLESIOSAURS RULE!

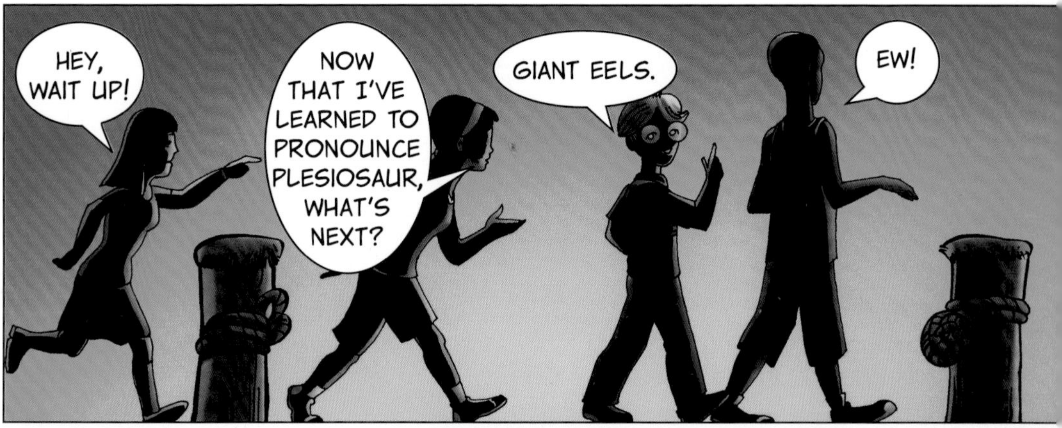
HEY, WAIT UP!
NOW THAT I'VE LEARNED TO PRONOUNCE PLESIOSAUR, WHAT'S NEXT?
GIANT EELS.
EW!

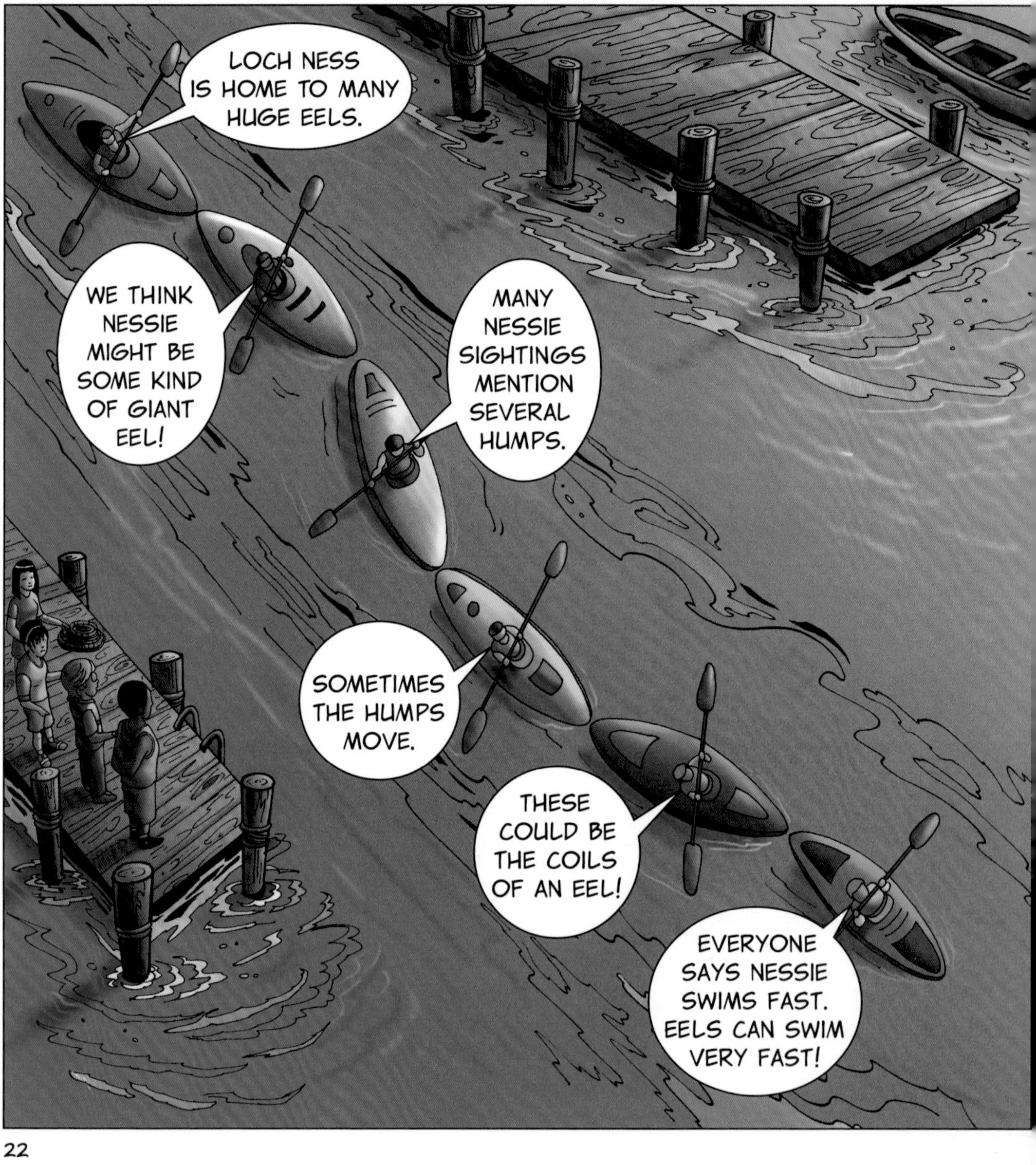
LOCH NESS IS HOME TO MANY HUGE EELS.
WE THINK NESSIE MIGHT BE SOME KIND OF GIANT EEL!
MANY NESSIE SIGHTINGS MENTION SEVERAL HUMPS.
SOMETIMES THE HUMPS MOVE.
THESE COULD BE THE COILS OF AN EEL!
EVERYONE SAYS NESSIE SWIMS FAST. EELS CAN SWIM VERY FAST!

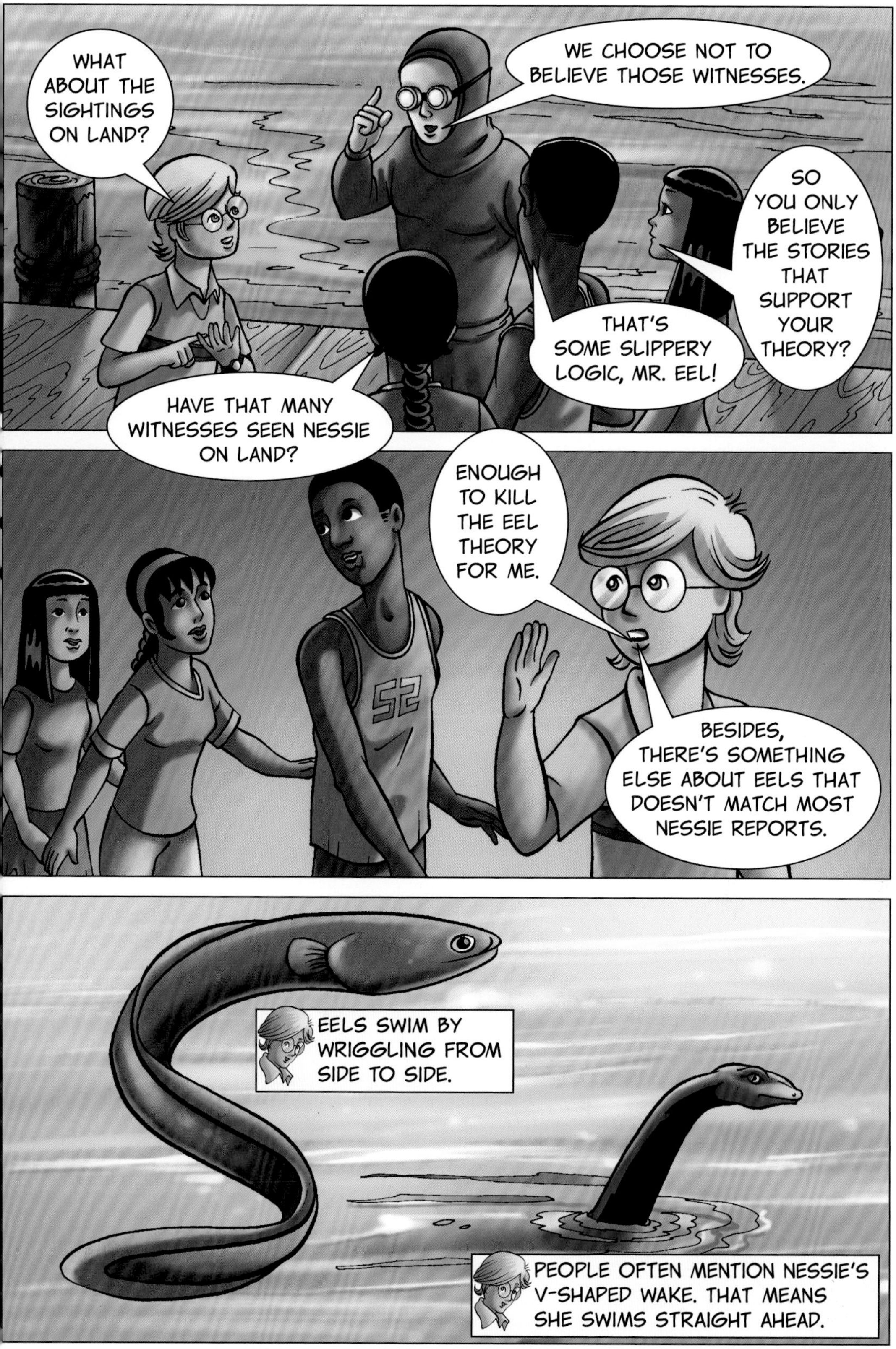
WHAT ABOUT THE SIGHTINGS ON LAND?
WE CHOOSE NOT TO BELIEVE THOSE WITNESSES.
SO YOU ONLY BELIEVE THE STORIES THAT SUPPORT YOUR THEORY?
THAT'S SOME SLIPPERY LOGIC, MR. EEL!
HAVE THAT MANY WITNESSES SEEN NESSIE ON LAND?
ENOUGH TO KILL THE EEL THEORY FOR ME.
BESIDES, THERE'S SOMETHING ELSE ABOUT EELS THAT DOESN'T MATCH MOST NESSIE REPORTS.
EELS SWIM BY WRIGGLING FROM SIDE TO SIDE.
PEOPLE OFTEN MENTION NESSIE'S V-SHAPED WAKE. THAT MEANS SHE SWIMS STRAIGHT AHEAD.

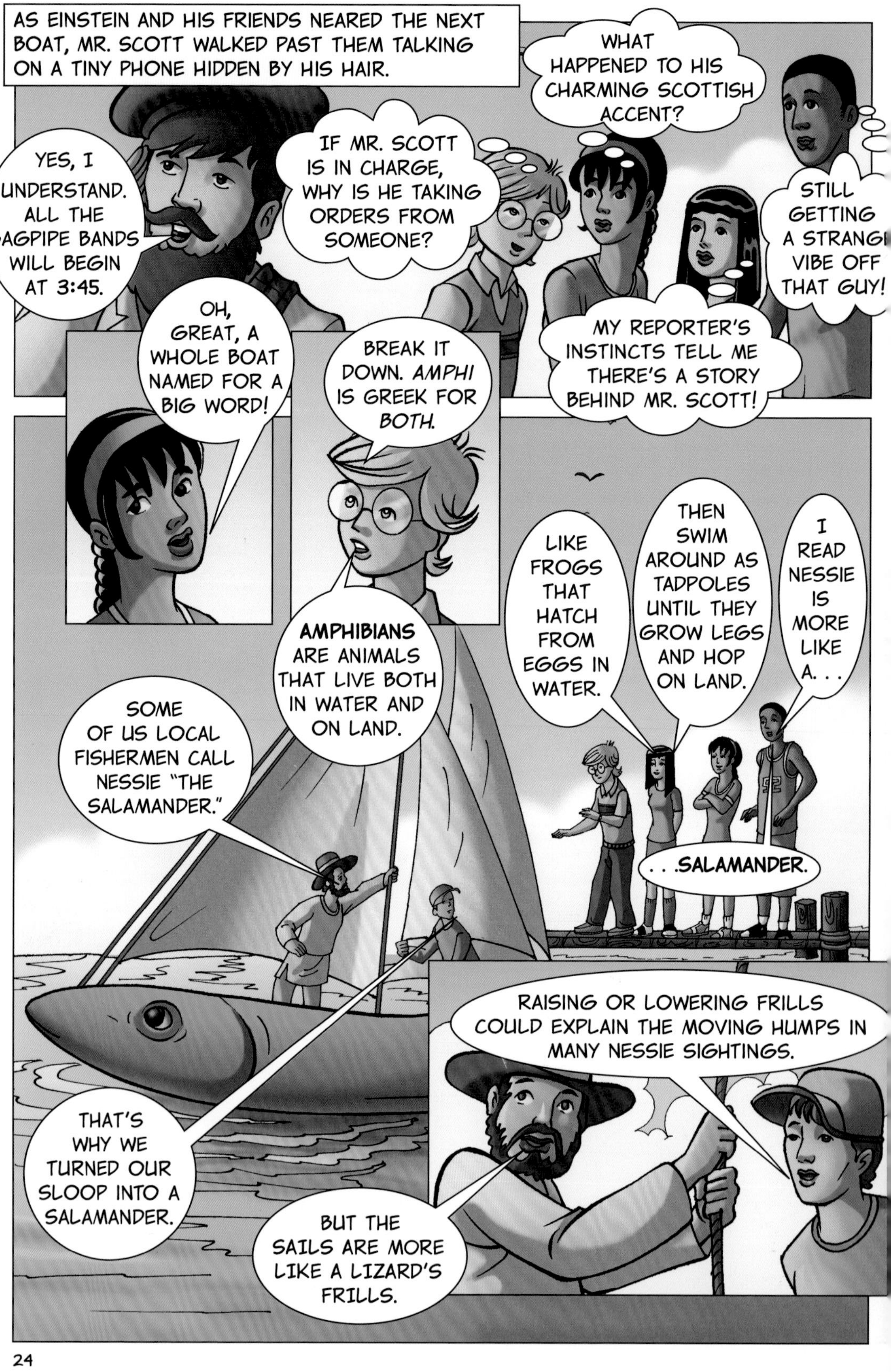
AS EINSTEIN AND HIS FRIENDS NEARED THE NEXT BOAT, MR. SCOTT WALKED PAST THEM TALKING ON A TINY PHONE HIDDEN BY HIS HAIR.
YES, I UNDERSTAND. ALL THE BAGPIPE BANDS WILL BEGIN AT 3:45.
IF MR. SCOTT IS IN CHARGE, WHY IS HE TAKING ORDERS FROM SOMEONE?
WHAT HAPPENED TO HIS CHARMING SCOTTISH ACCENT?
STILL GETTING A STRANGE VIBE OFF THAT GUY!
MY REPORTER'S INSTINCTS TELL ME THERE'S A STORY BEHIND MR. SCOTT!
OH, GREAT, A WHOLE BOAT NAMED FOR A BIG WORD!
BREAK IT DOWN. *AMPHI* IS GREEK FOR *BOTH*.
AMPHIBIANS ARE ANIMALS THAT LIVE BOTH IN WATER AND ON LAND.
LIKE FROGS THAT HATCH FROM EGGS IN WATER.
THEN SWIM AROUND AS TADPOLES UNTIL THEY GROW LEGS AND HOP ON LAND.
I READ NESSIE IS MORE LIKE A. . .
. . .SALAMANDER.
SOME OF US LOCAL FISHERMEN CALL NESSIE "THE SALAMANDER."
THAT'S WHY WE TURNED OUR SLOOP INTO A SALAMANDER.
BUT THE SAILS ARE MORE LIKE A LIZARD'S FRILLS.
RAISING OR LOWERING FRILLS COULD EXPLAIN THE MOVING HUMPS IN MANY NESSIE SIGHTINGS.

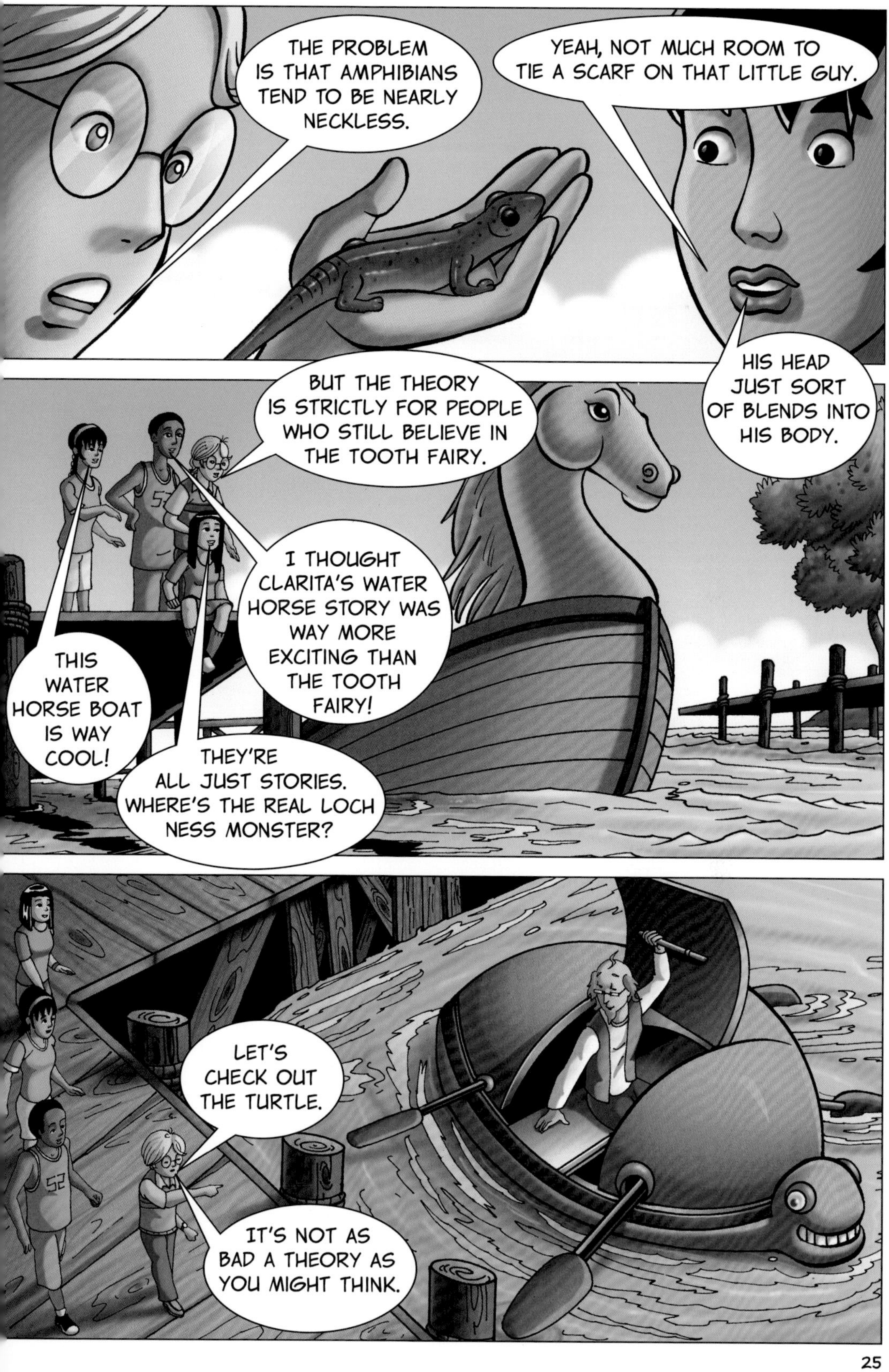
THE PROBLEM IS THAT AMPHIBIANS TEND TO BE NEARLY NECKLESS.
YEAH, NOT MUCH ROOM TO TIE A SCARF ON THAT LITTLE GUY.
HIS HEAD JUST SORT OF BLENDS INTO HIS BODY.
BUT THE THEORY IS STRICTLY FOR PEOPLE WHO STILL BELIEVE IN THE TOOTH FAIRY.
I THOUGHT CLARITA'S WATER HORSE STORY WAS WAY MORE EXCITING THAN THE TOOTH FAIRY!
THIS WATER HORSE BOAT IS WAY COOL!
THEY'RE ALL JUST STORIES. WHERE'S THE REAL LOCH NESS MONSTER?
LET'S CHECK OUT THE TURTLE.
IT'S NOT AS BAD A THEORY AS YOU MIGHT THINK.

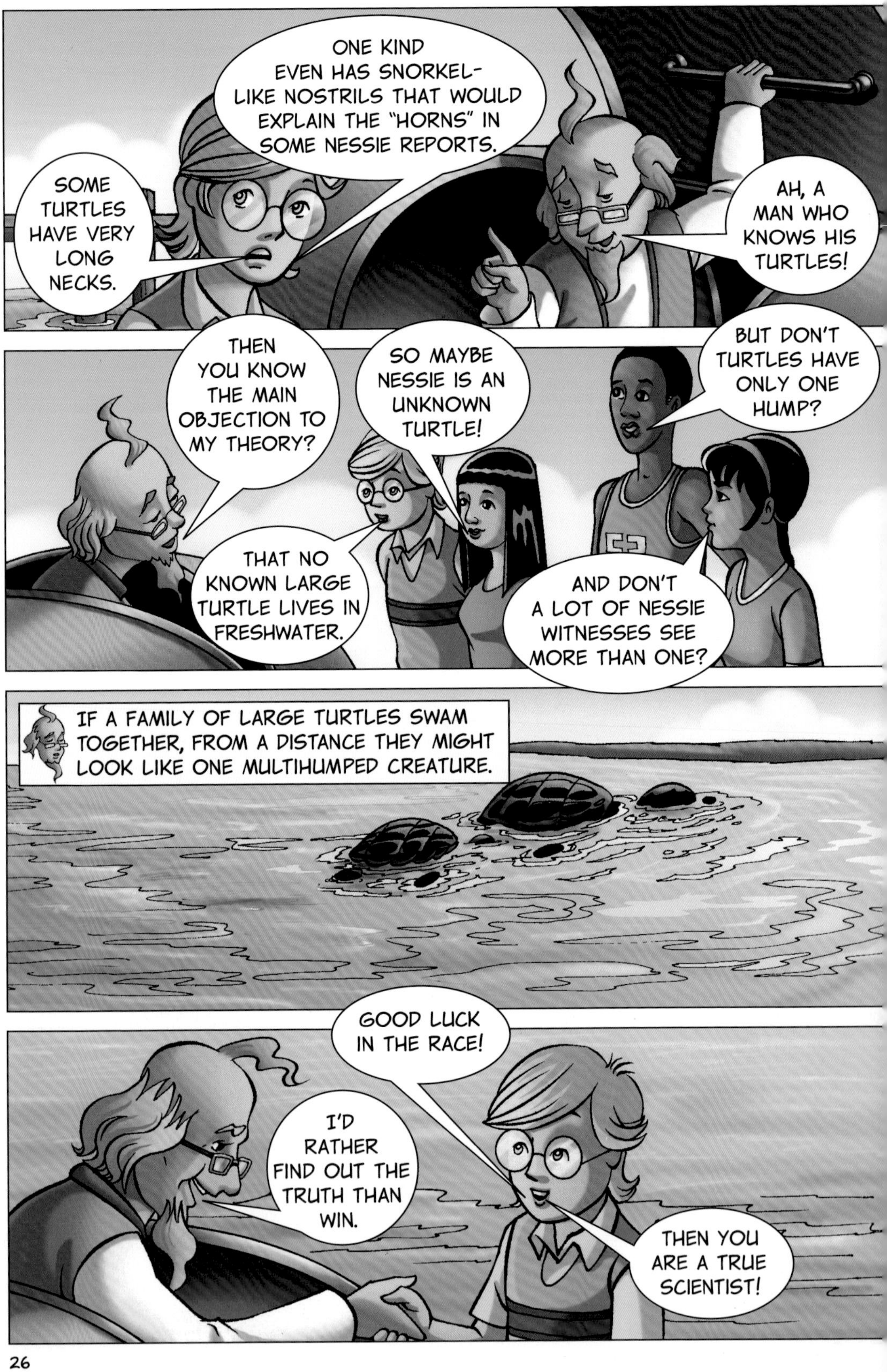
SOME TURTLES HAVE VERY LONG NECKS.
ONE KIND EVEN HAS SNORKEL-LIKE NOSTRILS THAT WOULD EXPLAIN THE "HORNS" IN SOME NESSIE REPORTS.
AH, A MAN WHO KNOWS HIS TURTLES!
THEN YOU KNOW THE MAIN OBJECTION TO MY THEORY?
THAT NO KNOWN LARGE TURTLE LIVES IN FRESHWATER.
SO MAYBE NESSIE IS AN UNKNOWN TURTLE!
BUT DON'T TURTLES HAVE ONLY ONE HUMP?
AND DON'T A LOT OF NESSIE WITNESSES SEE MORE THAN ONE?
IF A FAMILY OF LARGE TURTLES SWAM TOGETHER, FROM A DISTANCE THEY MIGHT LOOK LIKE ONE MULTIHUMPED CREATURE.
GOOD LUCK IN THE RACE!
I'D RATHER FIND OUT THE TRUTH THAN WIN.
THEN YOU ARE A TRUE SCIENTIST!

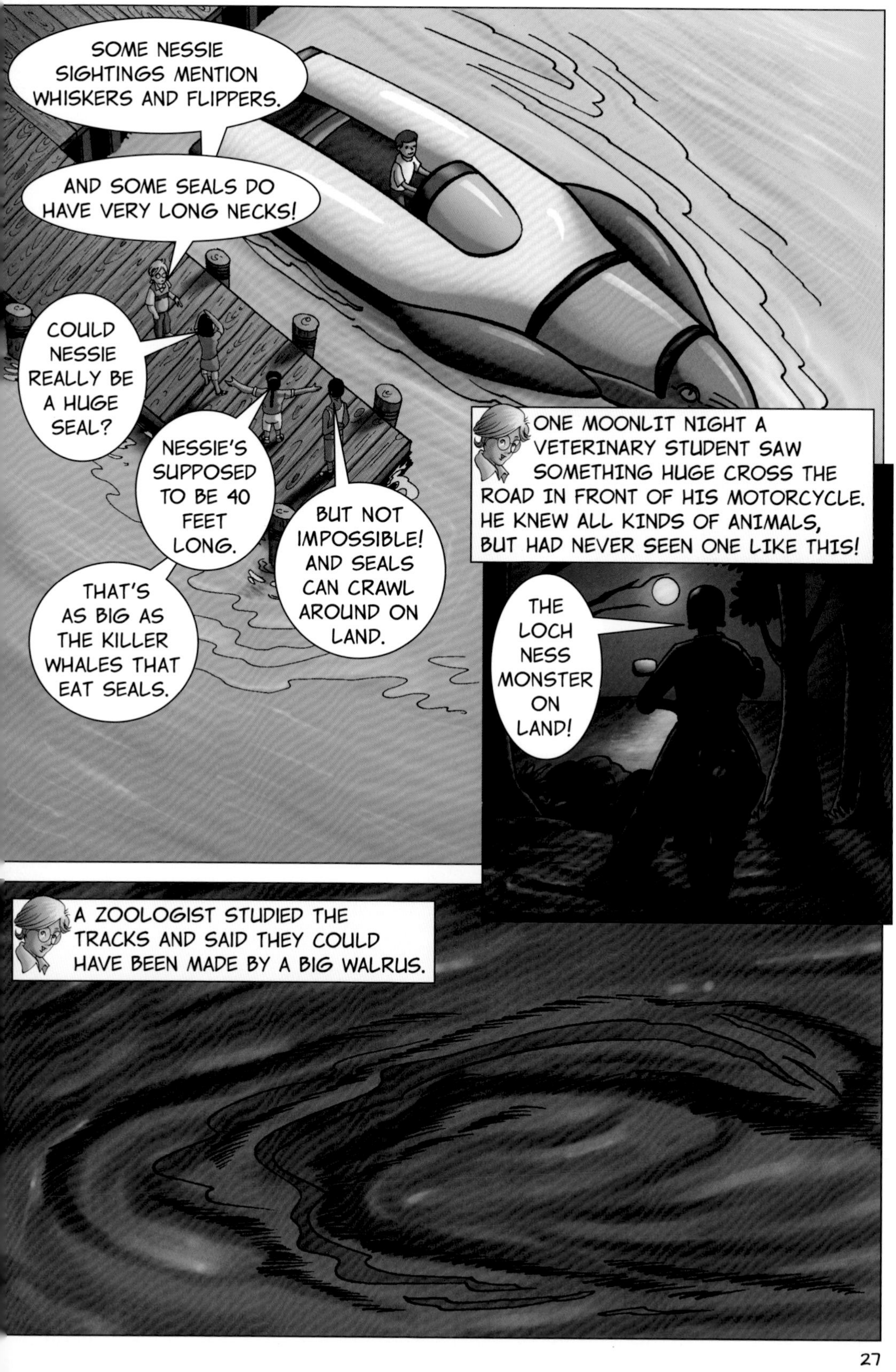
SOME NESSIE SIGHTINGS MENTION WHISKERS AND FLIPPERS.
AND SOME SEALS DO HAVE VERY LONG NECKS!
COULD NESSIE REALLY BE A HUGE SEAL?
NESSIE'S SUPPOSED TO BE 40 FEET LONG.
THAT'S AS BIG AS THE KILLER WHALES THAT EAT SEALS.
BUT NOT IMPOSSIBLE! AND SEALS CAN CRAWL AROUND ON LAND.
ONE MOONLIT NIGHT A VETERINARY STUDENT SAW SOMETHING HUGE CROSS THE ROAD IN FRONT OF HIS MOTORCYCLE. HE KNEW ALL KINDS OF ANIMALS, BUT HAD NEVER SEEN ONE LIKE THIS!
THE LOCH NESS MONSTER ON LAND!
A ZOOLOGIST STUDIED THE TRACKS AND SAID THEY COULD HAVE BEEN MADE BY A BIG WALRUS.

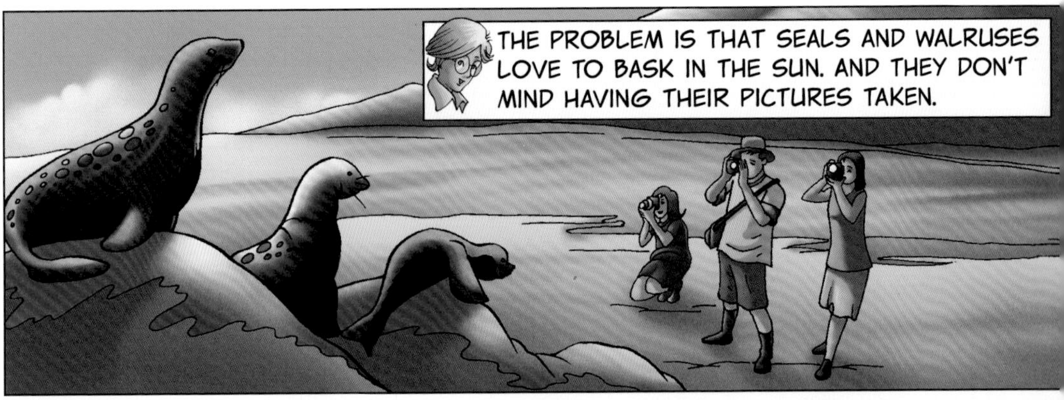
THE PROBLEM IS THAT SEALS AND WALRUSES LOVE TO BASK IN THE SUN. AND THEY DON'T MIND HAVING THEIR PICTURES TAKEN.

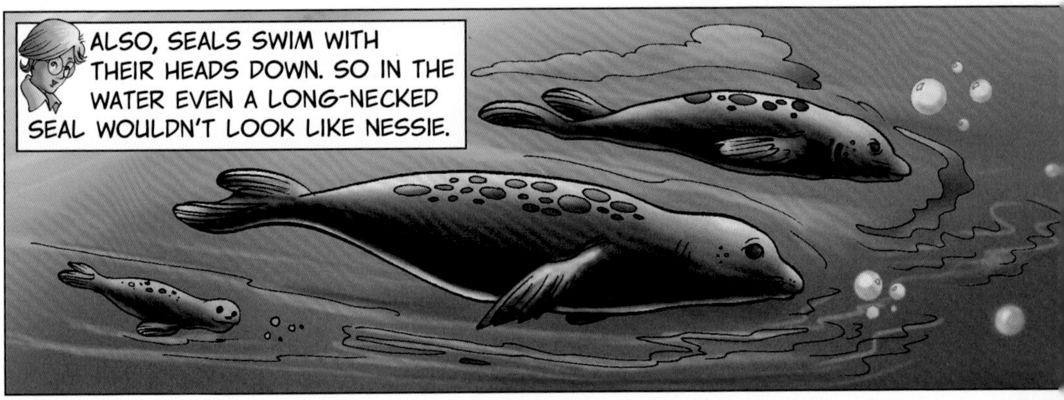
ALSO, SEALS SWIM WITH THEIR HEADS DOWN. SO IN THE WATER EVEN A LONG-NECKED SEAL WOULDN'T LOOK LIKE NESSIE.

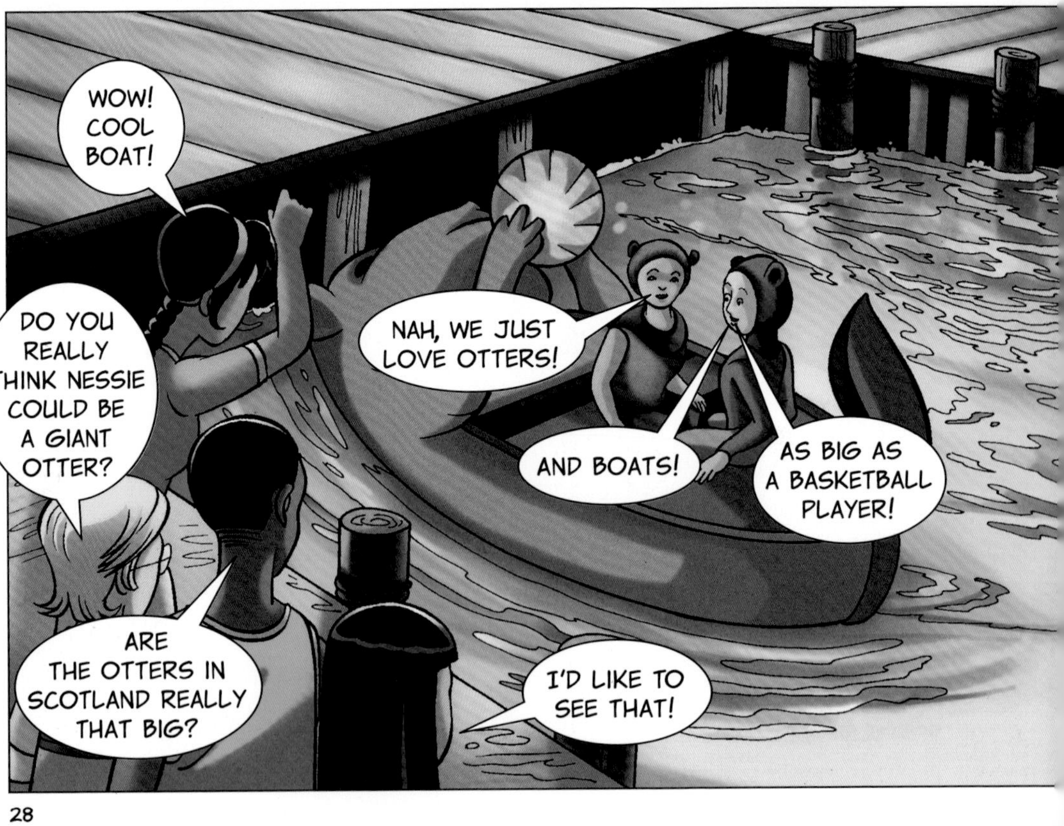
WOW! COOL BOAT!
NAH, WE JUST LOVE OTTERS!
AND BOATS!
DO YOU REALLY THINK NESSIE COULD BE A GIANT OTTER?
AS BIG AS A BASKETBALL PLAYER!
ARE THE OTTERS IN SCOTLAND REALLY THAT BIG?
I'D LIKE TO SEE THAT!

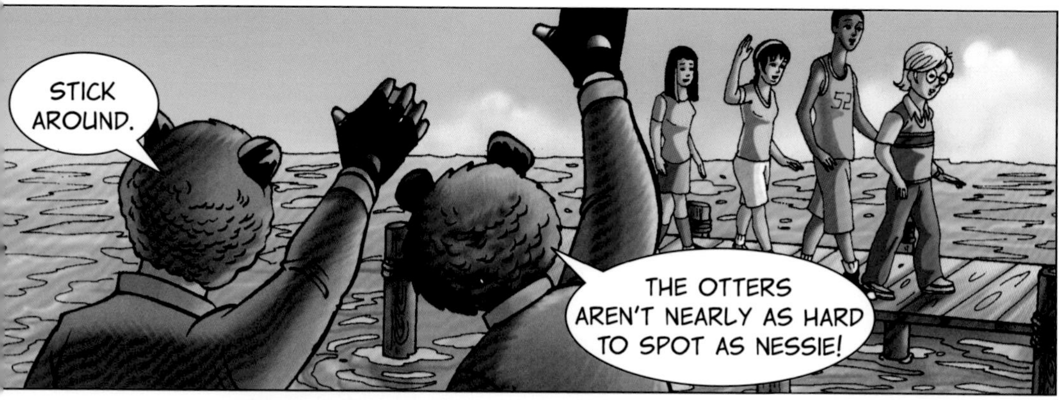
STICK AROUND.
THE OTTERS AREN'T NEARLY AS HARD TO SPOT AS NESSIE!

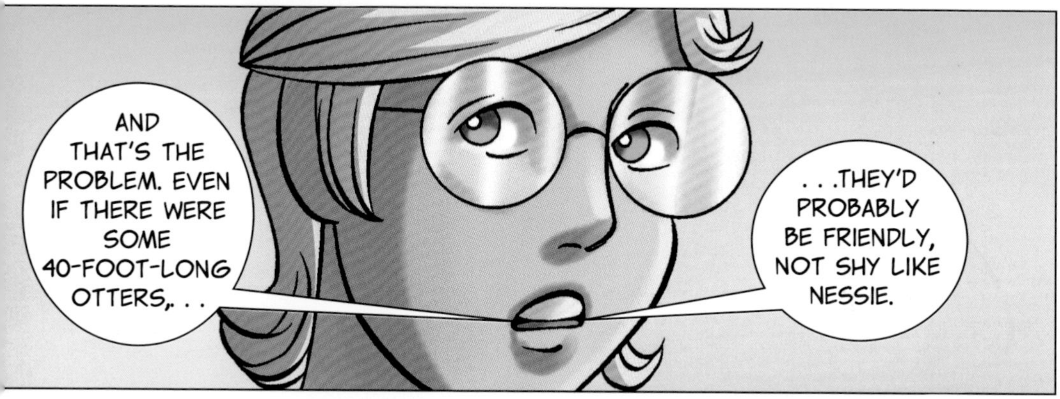
AND THAT'S THE PROBLEM. EVEN IF THERE WERE SOME 40-FOOT-LONG OTTERS,. . .
. . .THEY'D PROBABLY BE FRIENDLY, NOT SHY LIKE NESSIE.

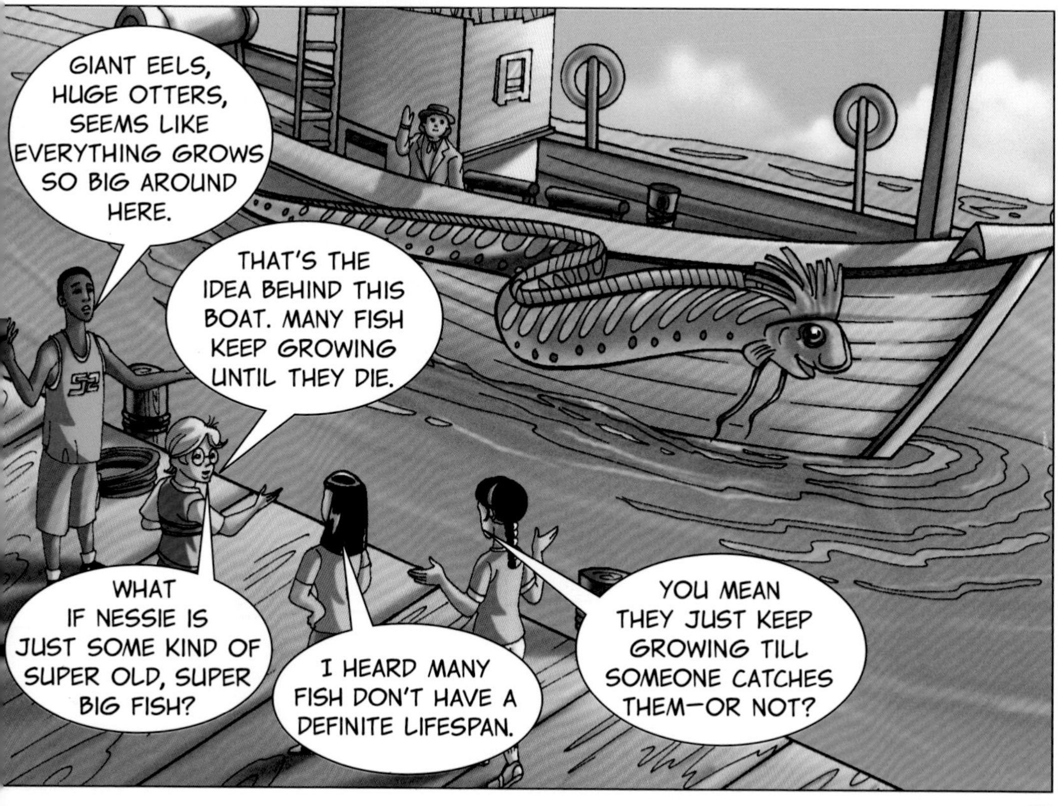
GIANT EELS, HUGE OTTERS, SEEMS LIKE EVERYTHING GROWS SO BIG AROUND HERE.
THAT'S THE IDEA BEHIND THIS BOAT. MANY FISH KEEP GROWING UNTIL THEY DIE.
WHAT IF NESSIE IS JUST SOME KIND OF SUPER OLD, SUPER BIG FISH?
I HEARD MANY FISH DON'T HAVE A DEFINITE LIFESPAN.
YOU MEAN THEY JUST KEEP GROWING TILL SOMEONE CATCHES THEM—OR NOT?

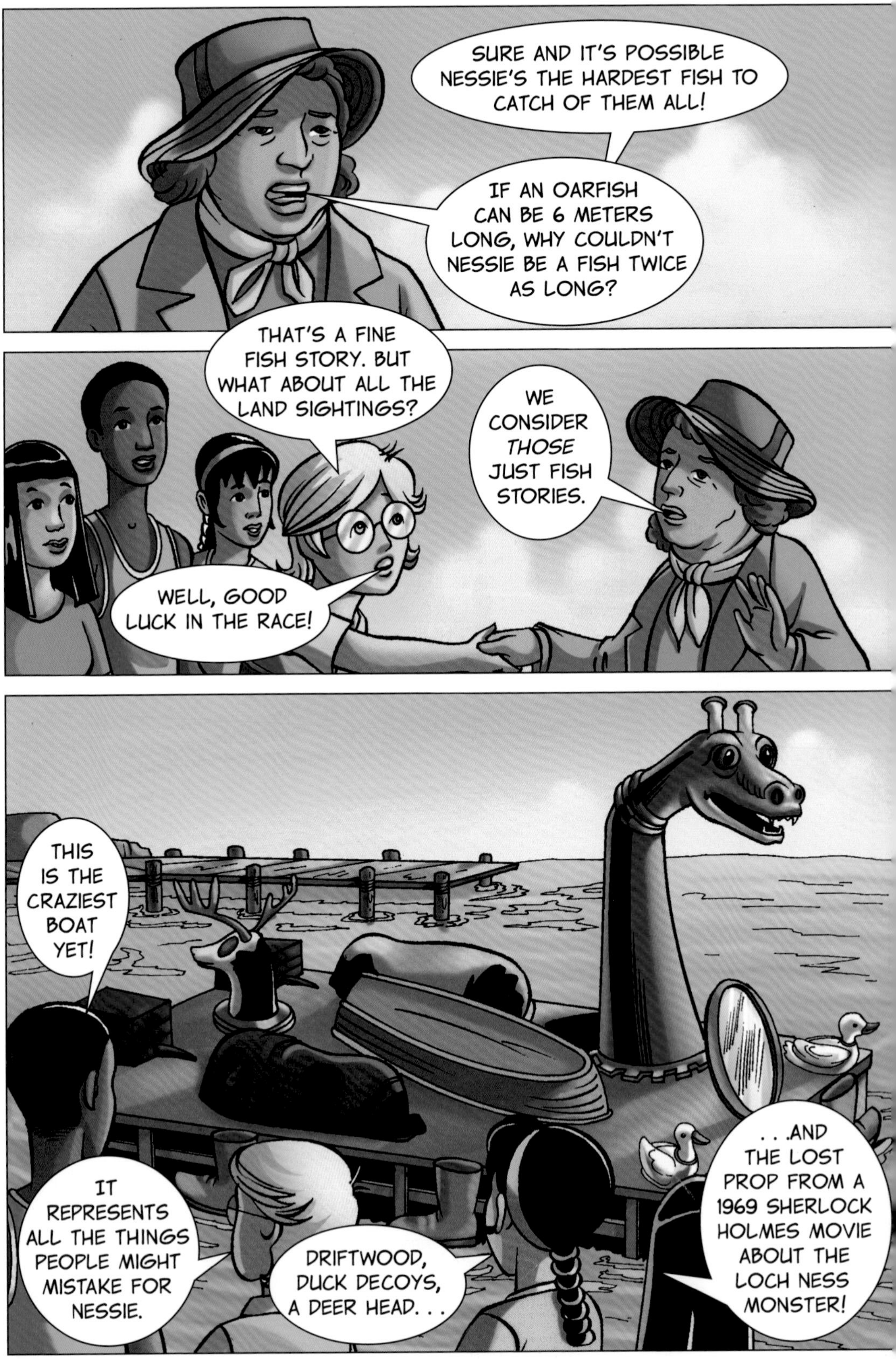
SURE AND IT'S POSSIBLE NESSIE'S THE HARDEST FISH TO CATCH OF THEM ALL!
IF AN OARFISH CAN BE 6 METERS LONG, WHY COULDN'T NESSIE BE A FISH TWICE AS LONG?
THAT'S A FINE FISH STORY. BUT WHAT ABOUT ALL THE LAND SIGHTINGS?
WE CONSIDER *THOSE* JUST FISH STORIES.
WELL, GOOD LUCK IN THE RACE!
THIS IS THE CRAZIEST BOAT YET!
IT REPRESENTS ALL THE THINGS PEOPLE MIGHT MISTAKE FOR NESSIE.
DRIFTWOOD, DUCK DECOYS, A DEER HEAD. . .
. . .AND THE LOST PROP FROM A 1969 SHERLOCK HOLMES MOVIE ABOUT THE LOCH NESS MONSTER!

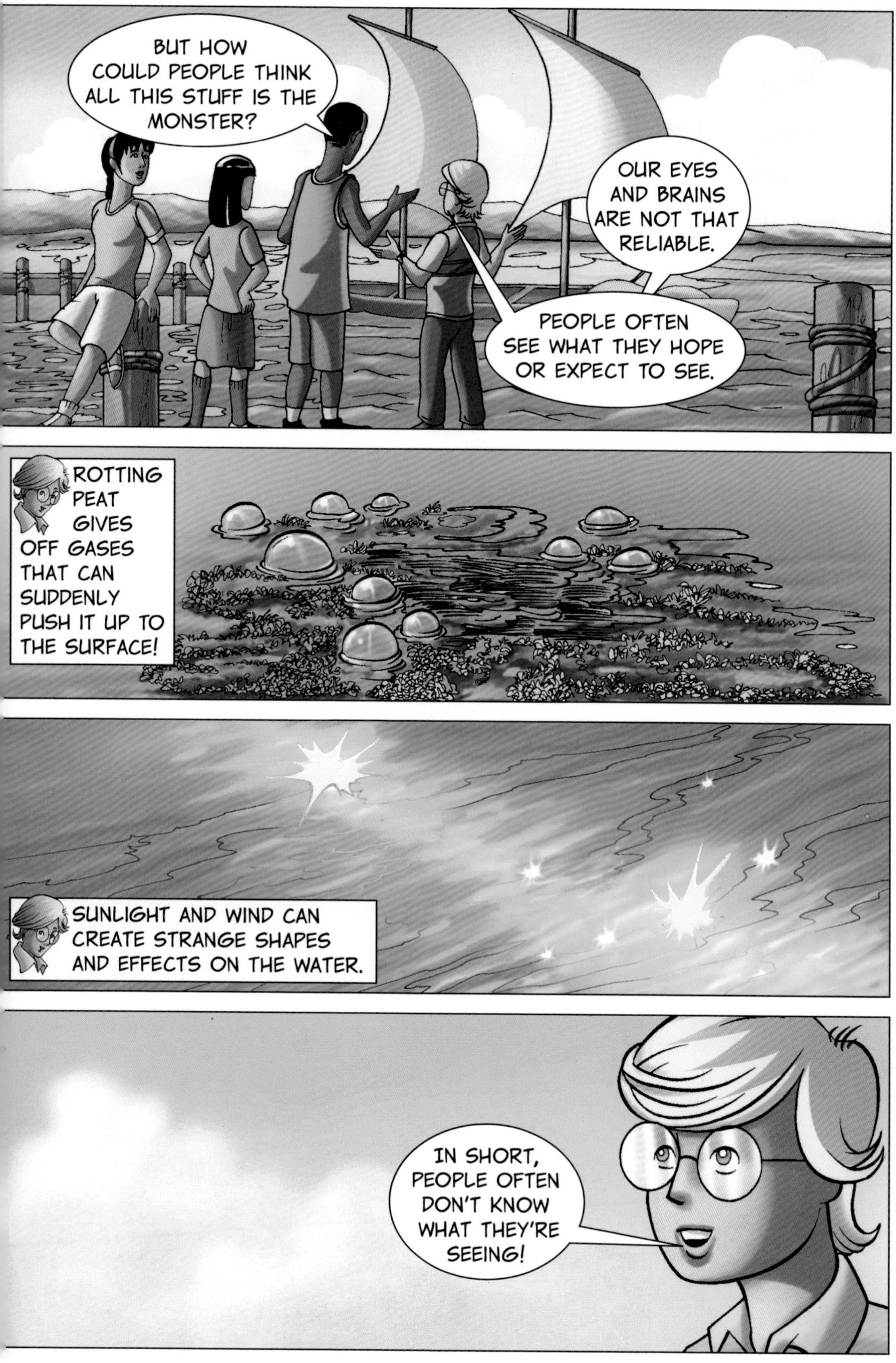
BUT HOW COULD PEOPLE THINK ALL THIS STUFF IS THE MONSTER?
OUR EYES AND BRAINS ARE NOT THAT RELIABLE.
PEOPLE OFTEN SEE WHAT THEY HOPE OR EXPECT TO SEE.
ROTTING PEAT GIVES OFF GASES THAT CAN SUDDENLY PUSH IT UP TO THE SURFACE!
SUNLIGHT AND WIND CAN CREATE STRANGE SHAPES AND EFFECTS ON THE WATER.
IN SHORT, PEOPLE OFTEN DON'T KNOW WHAT THEY'RE SEEING!

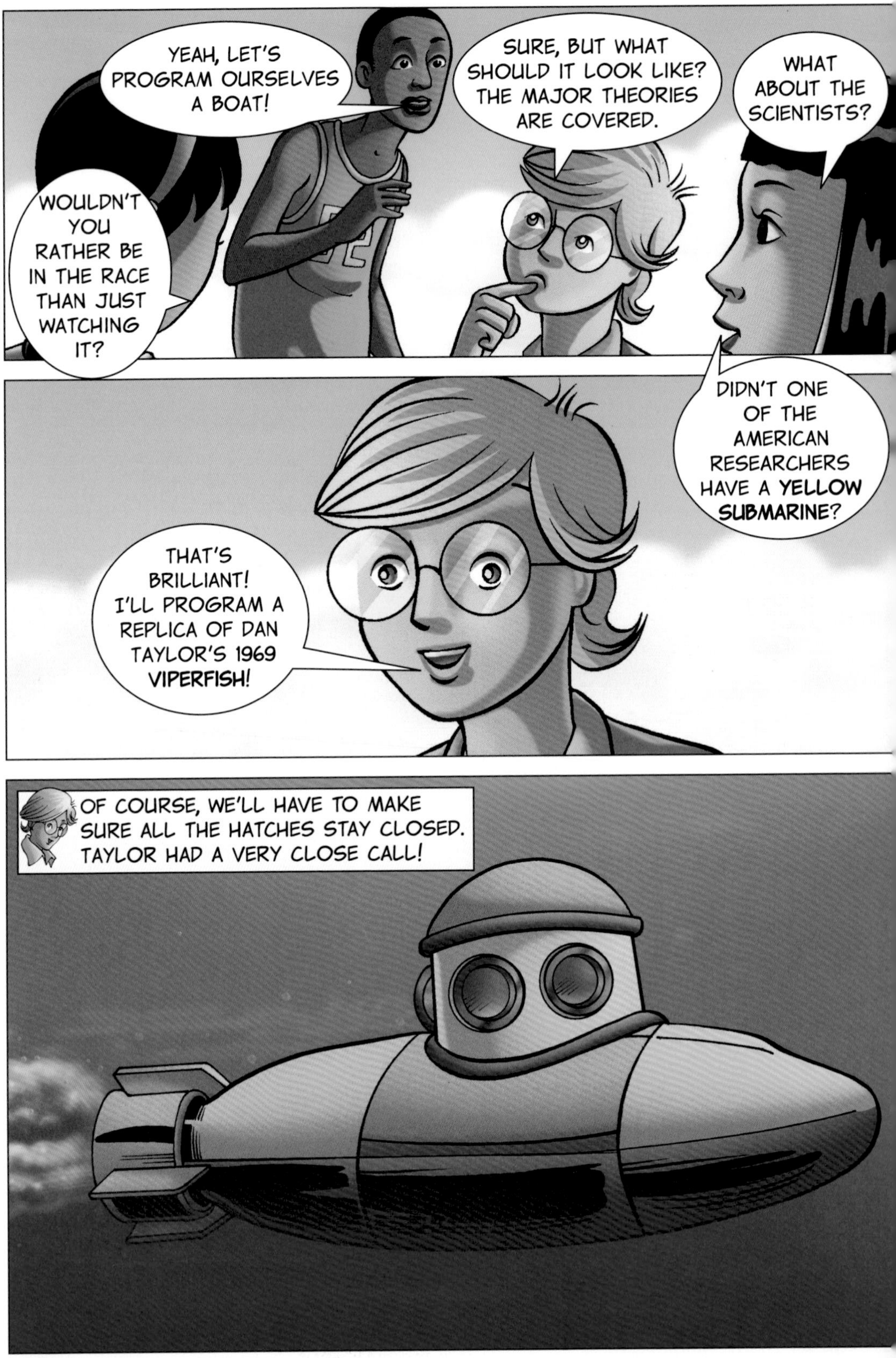

WOULDN'T YOU RATHER BE IN THE RACE THAN JUST WATCHING IT?
YEAH, LET'S PROGRAM OURSELVES A BOAT!
SURE, BUT WHAT SHOULD IT LOOK LIKE? THE MAJOR THEORIES ARE COVERED.
WHAT ABOUT THE SCIENTISTS?
DIDN'T ONE OF THE AMERICAN RESEARCHERS HAVE A **YELLOW SUBMARINE**?
THAT'S BRILLIANT! I'LL PROGRAM A REPLICA OF DAN TAYLOR'S 1969 **VIPERFISH**!
OF COURSE, WE'LL HAVE TO MAKE SURE ALL THE HATCHES STAY CLOSED. TAYLOR HAD A VERY CLOSE CALL!

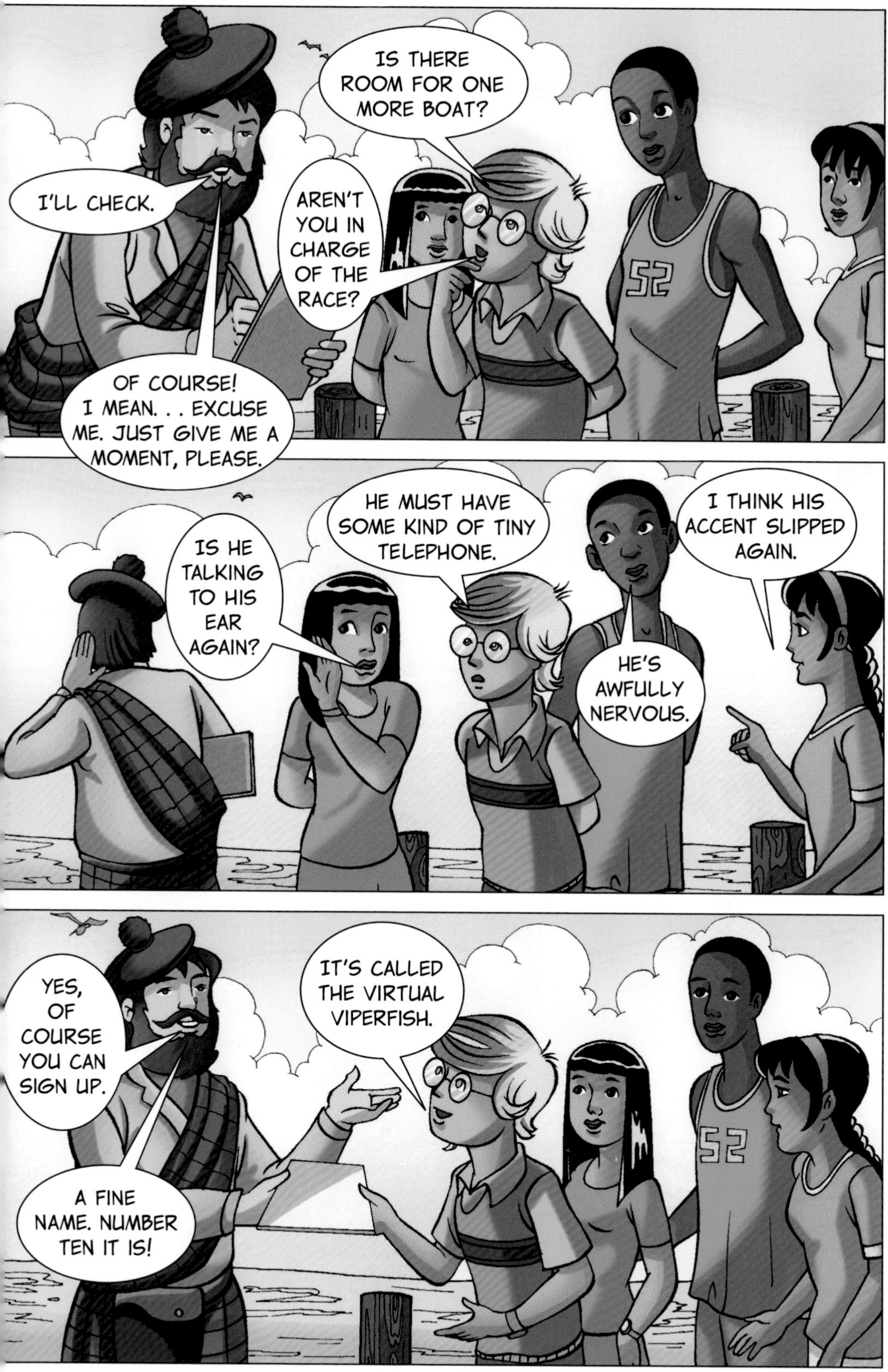
IS THERE ROOM FOR ONE MORE BOAT?
I'LL CHECK.
AREN'T YOU IN CHARGE OF THE RACE?
OF COURSE! I MEAN. . . EXCUSE ME. JUST GIVE ME A MOMENT, PLEASE.
IS HE TALKING TO HIS EAR AGAIN?
HE MUST HAVE SOME KIND OF TINY TELEPHONE.
HE'S AWFULLY NERVOUS.
I THINK HIS ACCENT SLIPPED AGAIN.
YES, OF COURSE YOU CAN SIGN UP.
IT'S CALLED THE VIRTUAL VIPERFISH.
A FINE NAME. NUMBER TEN IT IS!

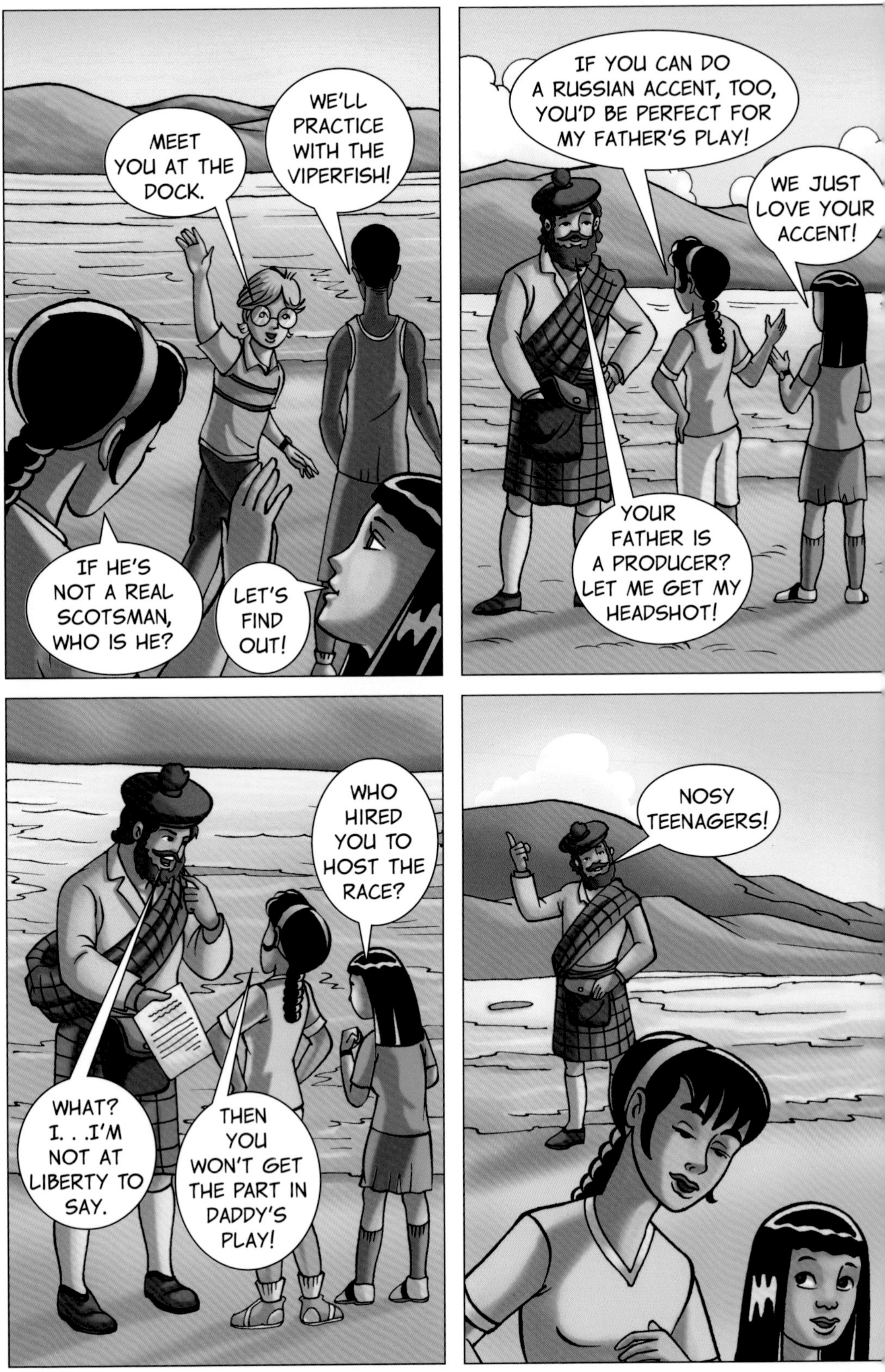
MEET YOU AT THE DOCK.
WE'LL PRACTICE WITH THE VIPERFISH!
IF HE'S NOT A REAL SCOTSMAN, WHO IS HE?
LET'S FIND OUT!
IF YOU CAN DO A RUSSIAN ACCENT, TOO, YOU'D BE PERFECT FOR MY FATHER'S PLAY!
WE JUST LOVE YOUR ACCENT!
YOUR FATHER IS A PRODUCER? LET ME GET MY HEADSHOT!
WHO HIRED YOU TO HOST THE RACE?
WHAT? I. . .I'M NOT AT LIBERTY TO SAY.
THEN YOU WON'T GET THE PART IN DADDY'S PLAY!
NOSY TEENAGERS!

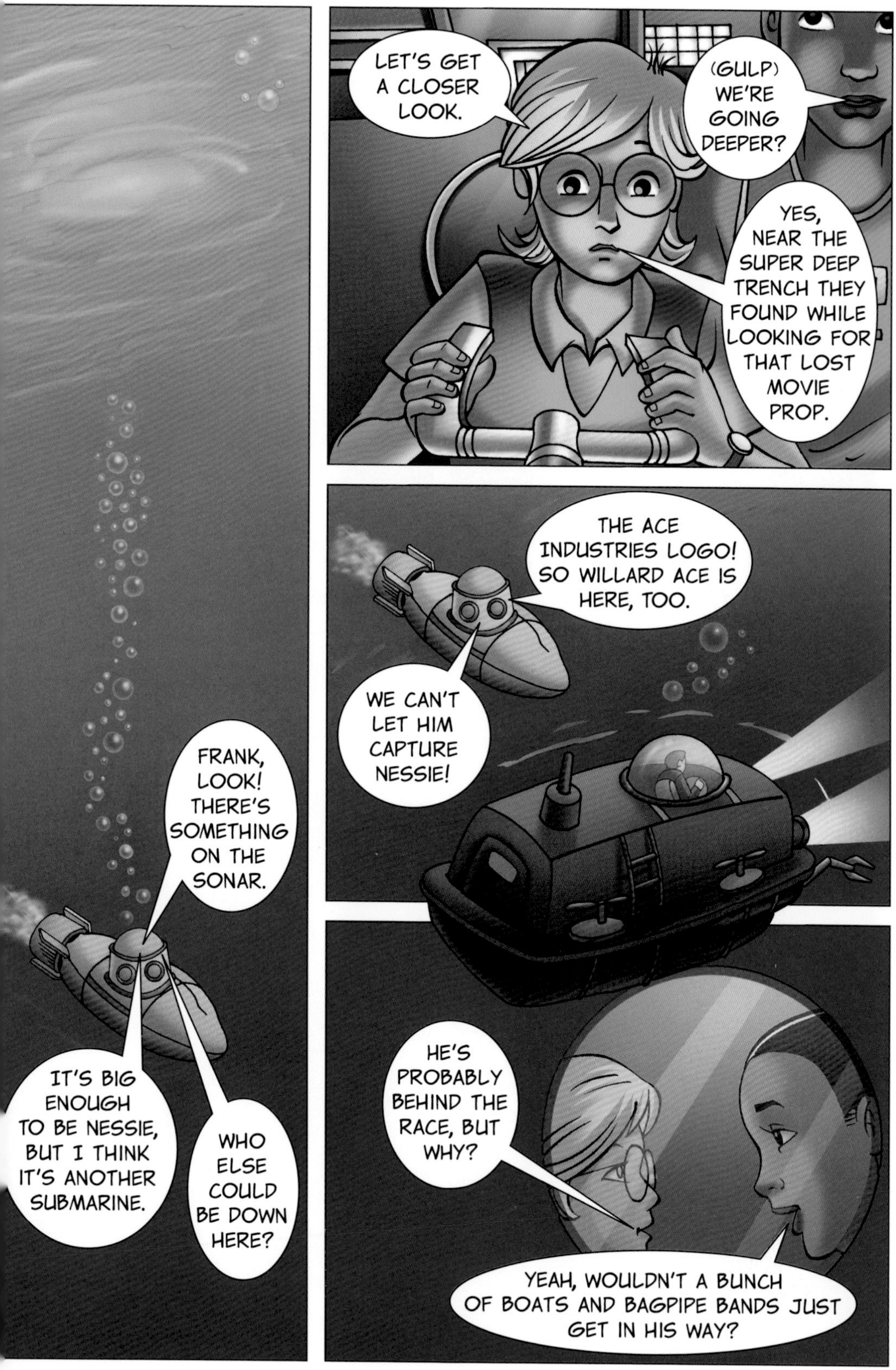
FRANK, LOOK! THERE'S SOMETHING ON THE SONAR.
IT'S BIG ENOUGH TO BE NESSIE, BUT I THINK IT'S ANOTHER SUBMARINE.
WHO ELSE COULD BE DOWN HERE?
LET'S GET A CLOSER LOOK.
(GULP) WE'RE GOING DEEPER?
YES, NEAR THE SUPER DEEP TRENCH THEY FOUND WHILE LOOKING FOR THAT LOST MOVIE PROP.
THE ACE INDUSTRIES LOGO! SO WILLARD ACE IS HERE, TOO.
WE CAN'T LET HIM CAPTURE NESSIE!
HE'S PROBABLY BEHIND THE RACE, BUT WHY?
YEAH, WOULDN'T A BUNCH OF BOATS AND BAGPIPE BANDS JUST GET IN HIS WAY?

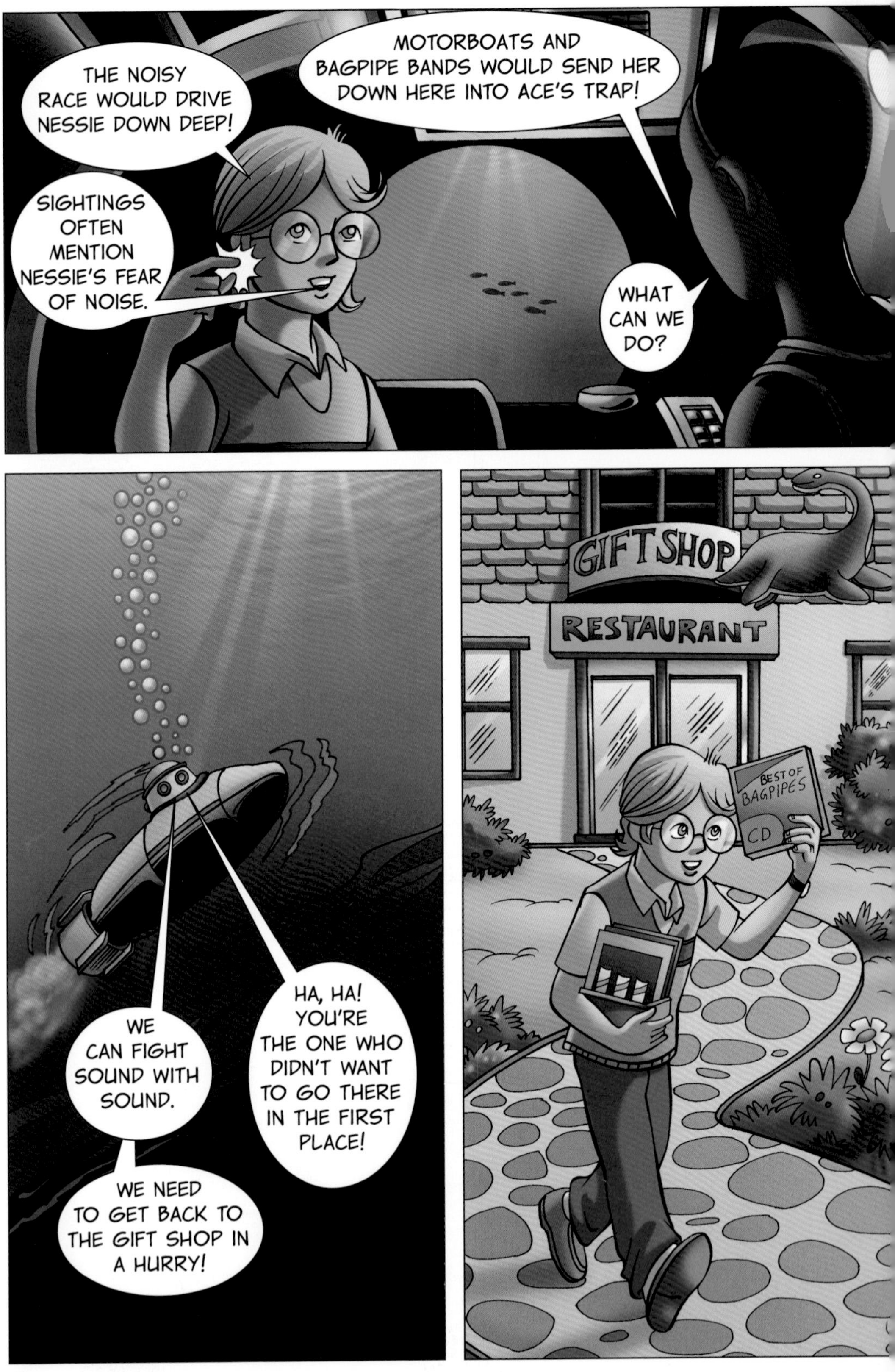
THE NOISY RACE WOULD DRIVE NESSIE DOWN DEEP!
SIGHTINGS OFTEN MENTION NESSIE'S FEAR OF NOISE.
MOTORBOATS AND BAGPIPE BANDS WOULD SEND HER DOWN HERE INTO ACE'S TRAP!
WHAT CAN WE DO?
WE CAN FIGHT SOUND WITH SOUND.
WE NEED TO GET BACK TO THE GIFT SHOP IN A HURRY!
HA, HA! YOU'RE THE ONE WHO DIDN'T WANT TO GO THERE IN THE FIRST PLACE!
GIFT SHOP
RESTAURANT
BEST OF BAGPIPES
CD

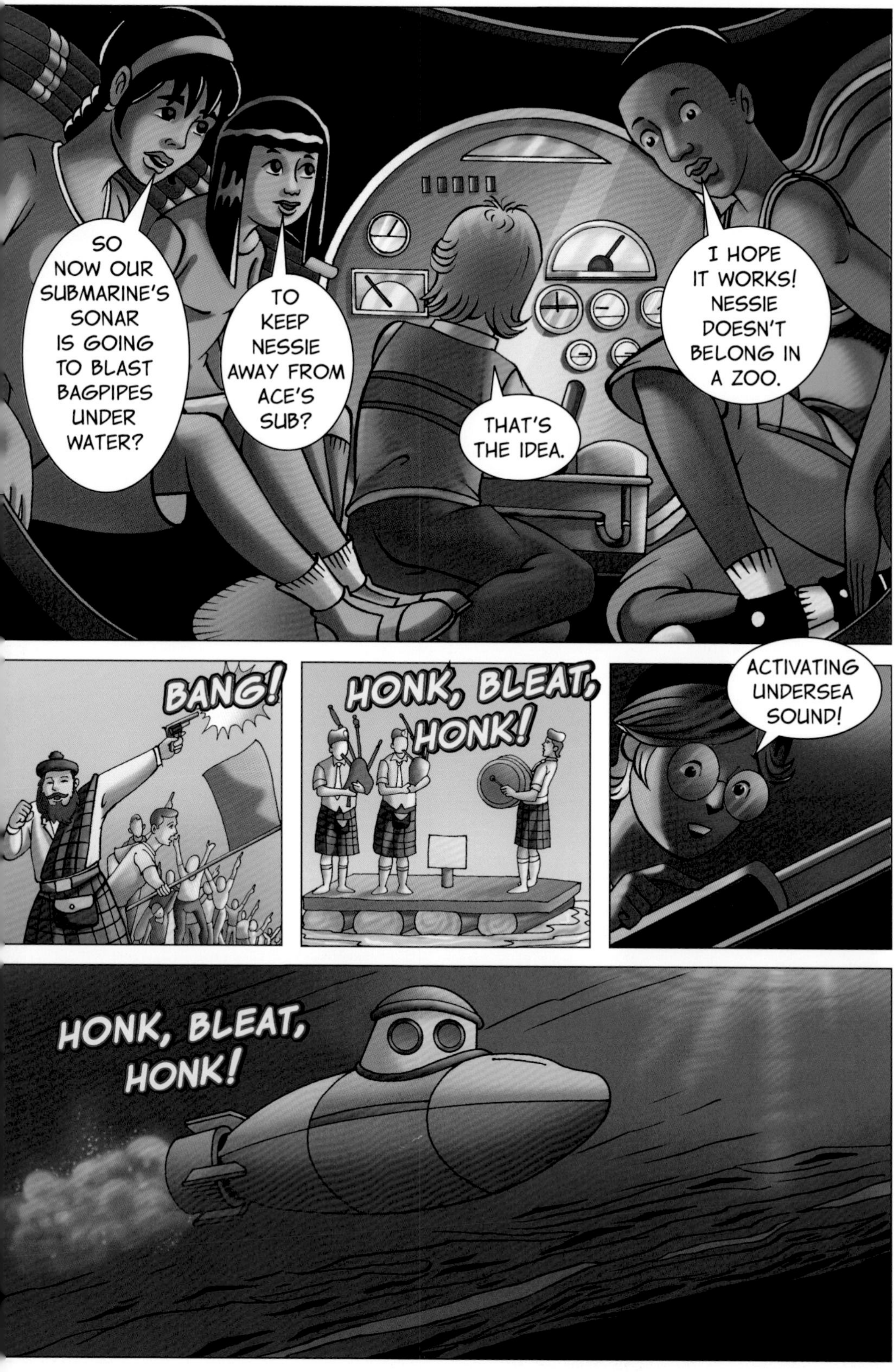
SO NOW OUR SUBMARINE'S SONAR IS GOING TO BLAST BAGPIPES UNDER WATER?
TO KEEP NESSIE AWAY FROM ACE'S SUB?
THAT'S THE IDEA.
I HOPE IT WORKS! NESSIE DOESN'T BELONG IN A ZOO.
BANG!
HONK, BLEAT, HONK!
ACTIVATING UNDERSEA SOUND!
HONK, BLEAT, HONK!

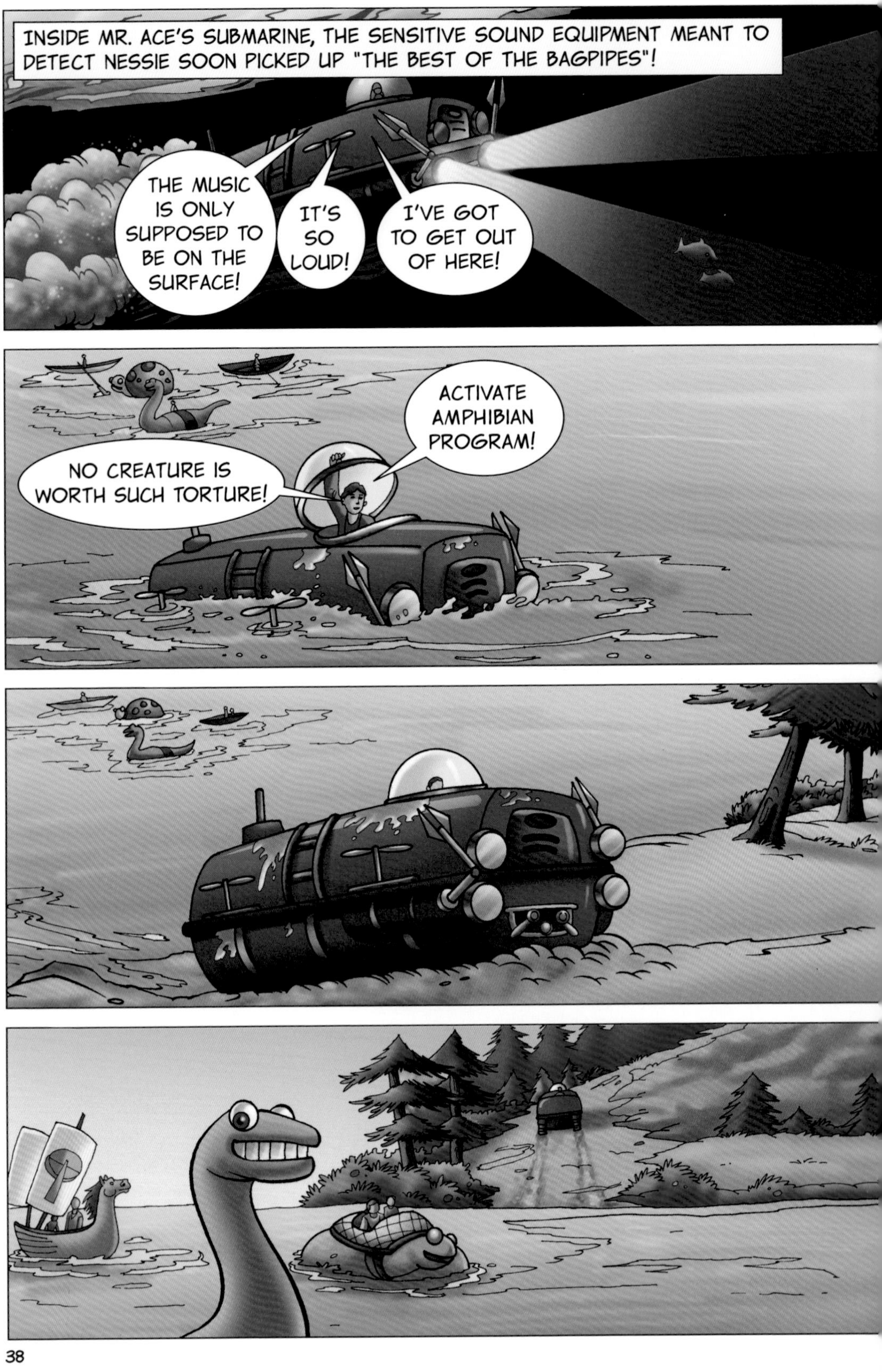
INSIDE MR. ACE'S SUBMARINE, THE SENSITIVE SOUND EQUIPMENT MEANT TO DETECT NESSIE SOON PICKED UP "THE BEST OF THE BAGPIPES"!
THE MUSIC IS ONLY SUPPOSED TO BE ON THE SURFACE!
IT'S SO LOUD!
I'VE GOT TO GET OUT OF HERE!
ACTIVATE AMPHIBIAN PROGRAM!
NO CREATURE IS WORTH SUCH TORTURE!

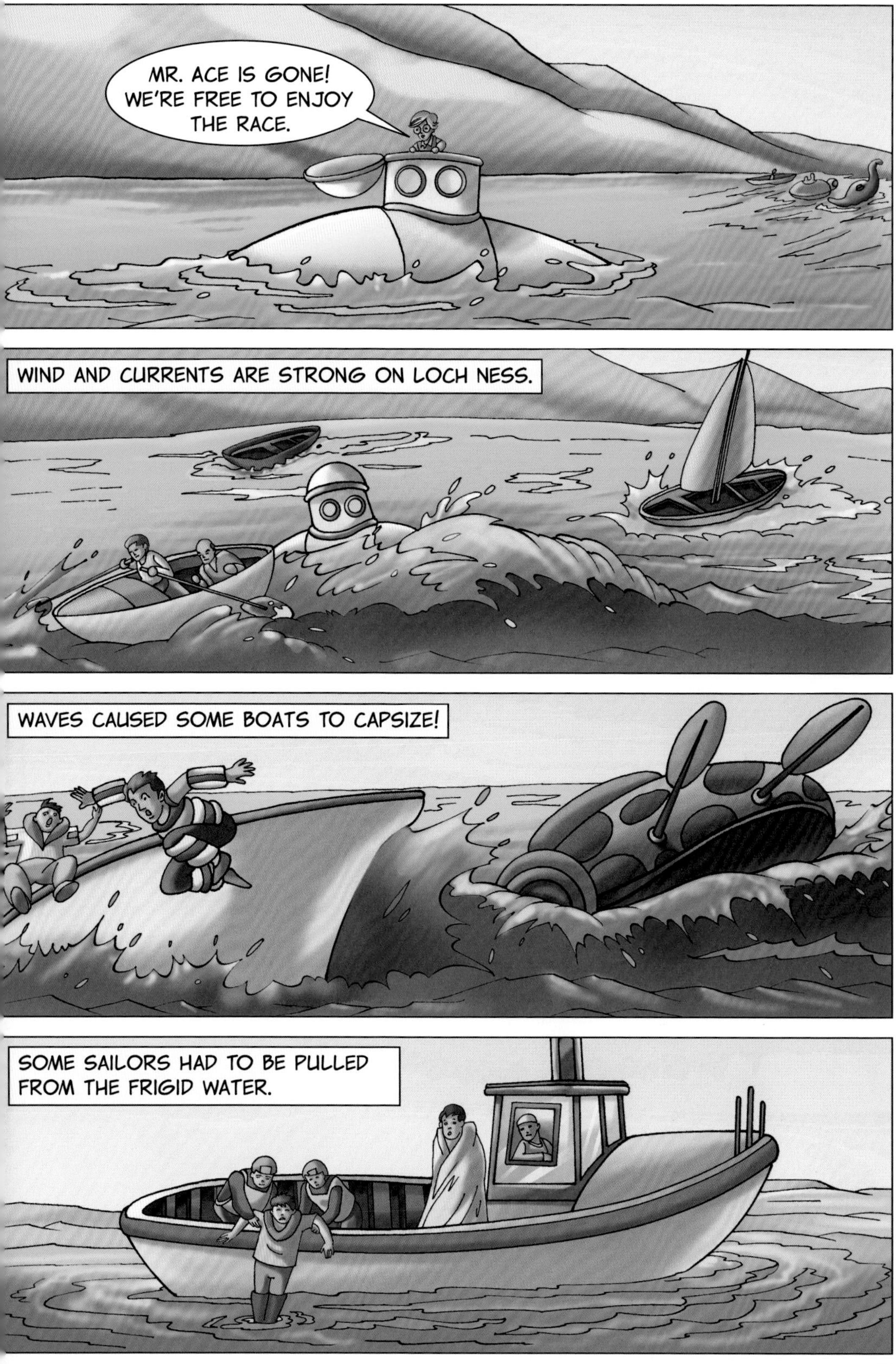
MR. ACE IS GONE! WE'RE FREE TO ENJOY THE RACE.
WIND AND CURRENTS ARE STRONG ON LOCH NESS.
WAVES CAUSED SOME BOATS TO CAPSIZE!
SOME SAILORS HAD TO BE PULLED FROM THE FRIGID WATER.

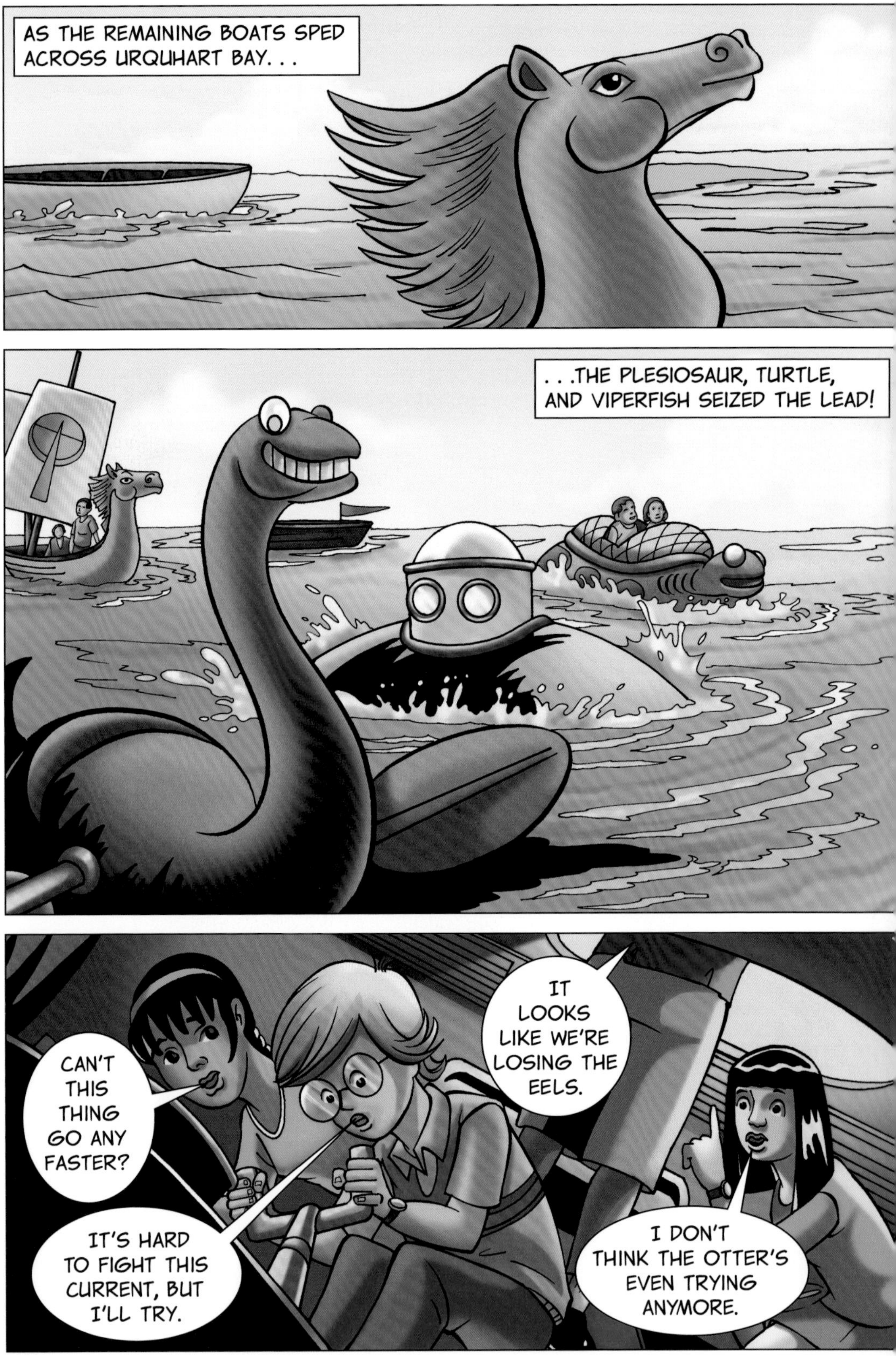
AS THE REMAINING BOATS SPED ACROSS URQUHART BAY. . .
. . .THE PLESIOSAUR, TURTLE, AND VIPERFISH SEIZED THE LEAD!
CAN'T THIS THING GO ANY FASTER?
IT'S HARD TO FIGHT THIS CURRENT, BUT I'LL TRY.
IT LOOKS LIKE WE'RE LOSING THE EELS.
I DON'T THINK THE OTTER'S EVEN TRYING ANYMORE.

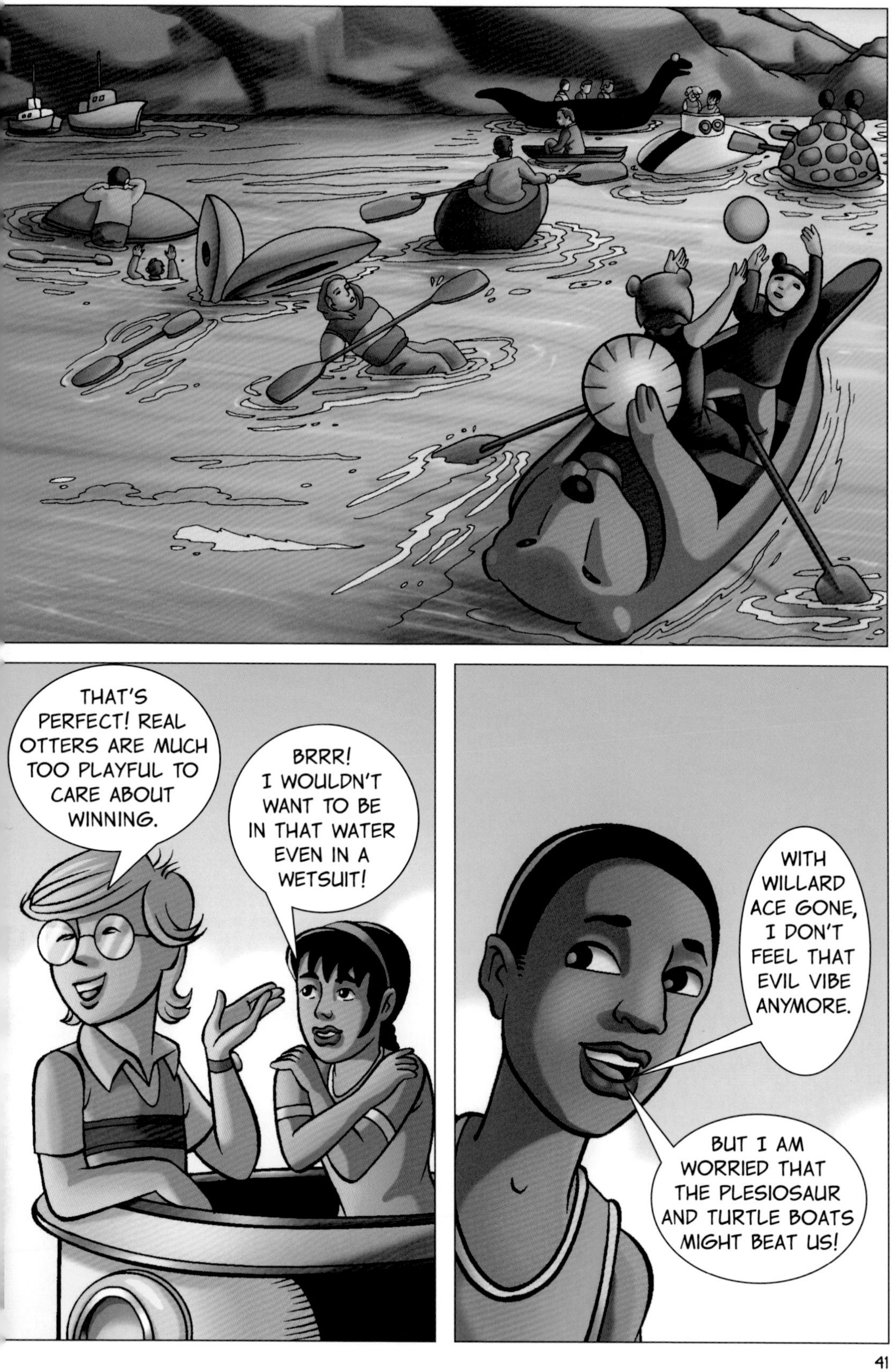
THAT'S PERFECT! REAL OTTERS ARE MUCH TOO PLAYFUL TO CARE ABOUT WINNING.
BRRR! I WOULDN'T WANT TO BE IN THAT WATER EVEN IN A WETSUIT!
WITH WILLARD ACE GONE, I DON'T FEEL THAT EVIL VIBE ANYMORE.
BUT I AM WORRIED THAT THE PLESIOSAUR AND TURTLE BOATS MIGHT BEAT US!

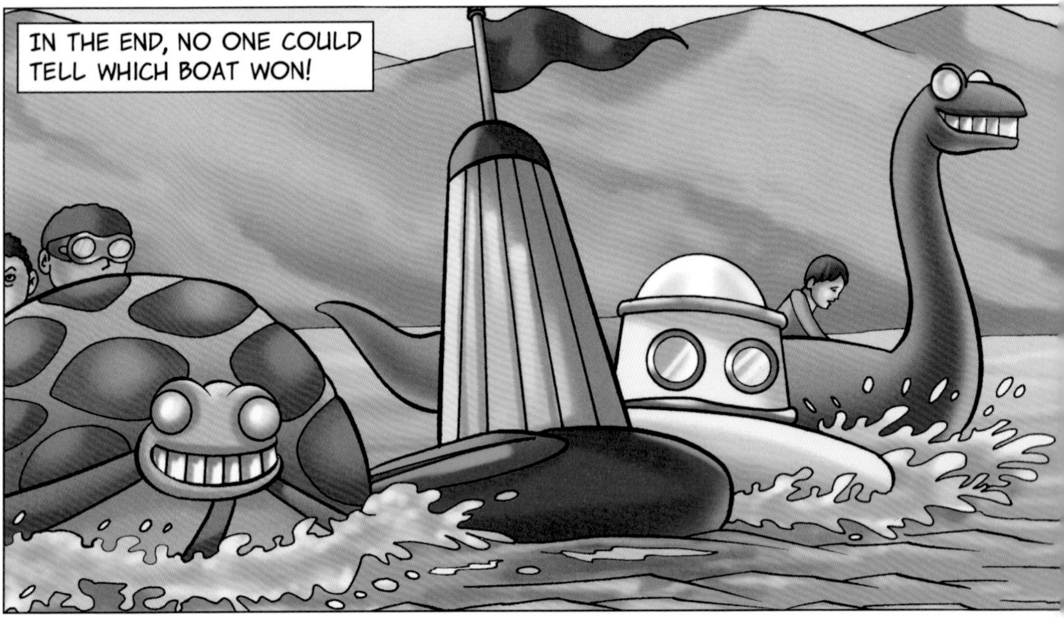
IN THE END, NO ONE COULD TELL WHICH BOAT WON!

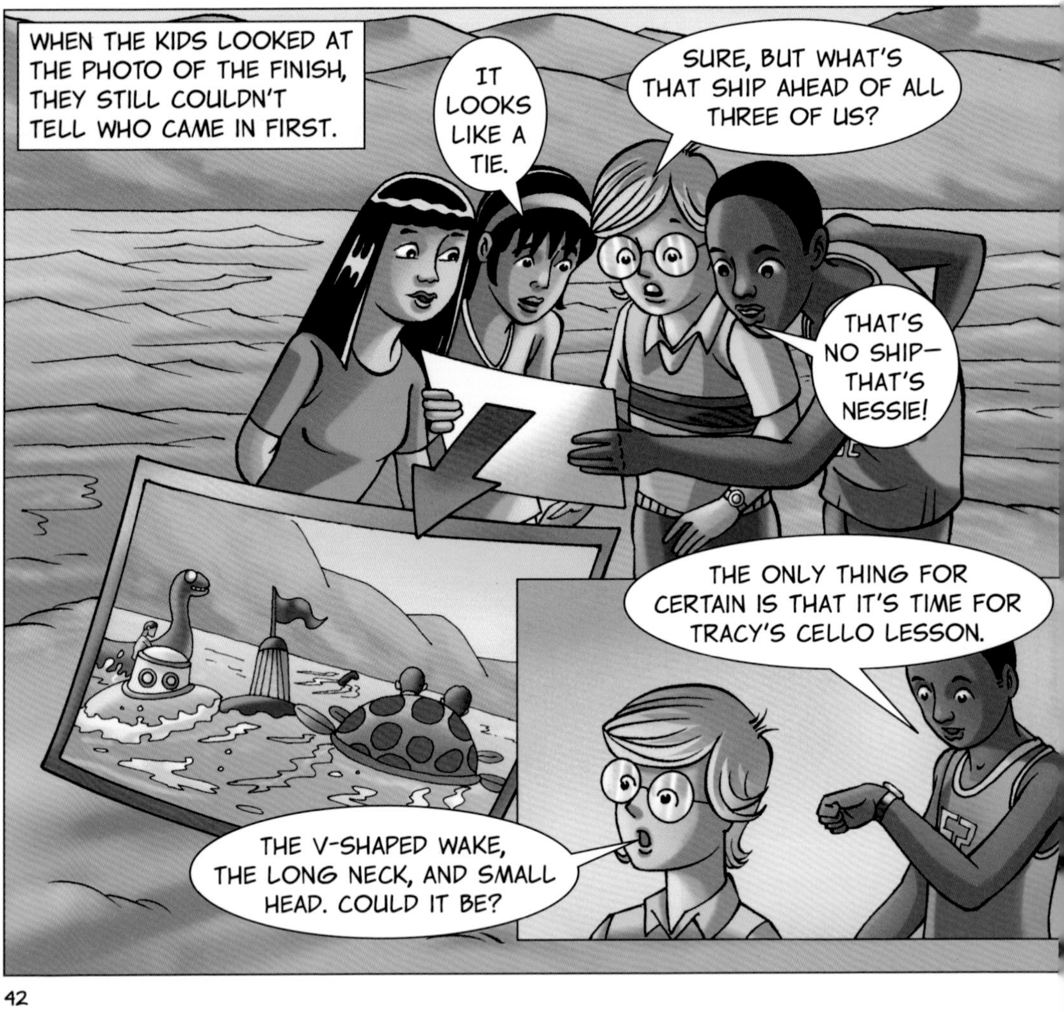
WHEN THE KIDS LOOKED AT THE PHOTO OF THE FINISH, THEY STILL COULDN'T TELL WHO CAME IN FIRST.
IT LOOKS LIKE A TIE.
SURE, BUT WHAT'S THAT SHIP AHEAD OF ALL THREE OF US?
THAT'S NO SHIP— THAT'S NESSIE!
THE V-SHAPED WAKE, THE LONG NECK, AND SMALL HEAD. COULD IT BE?
THE ONLY THING FOR CERTAIN IS THAT IT'S TIME FOR TRACY'S CELLO LESSON.

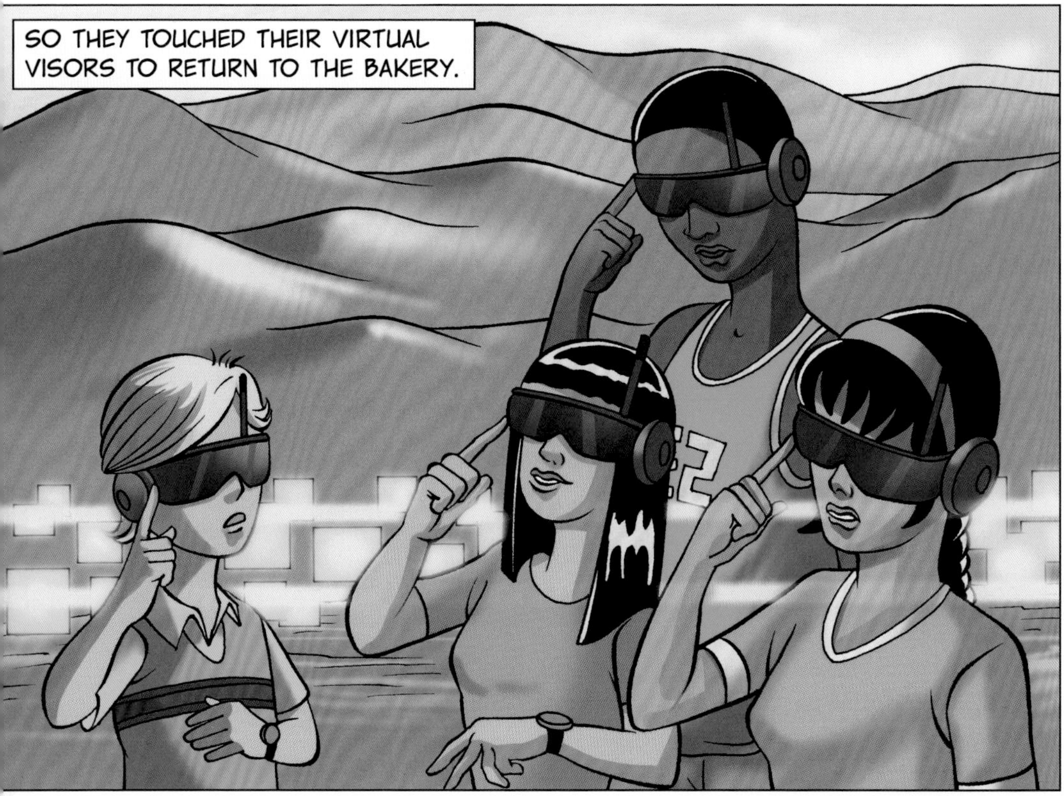
SO THEY TOUCHED THEIR VIRTUAL VISORS TO RETURN TO THE BAKERY.

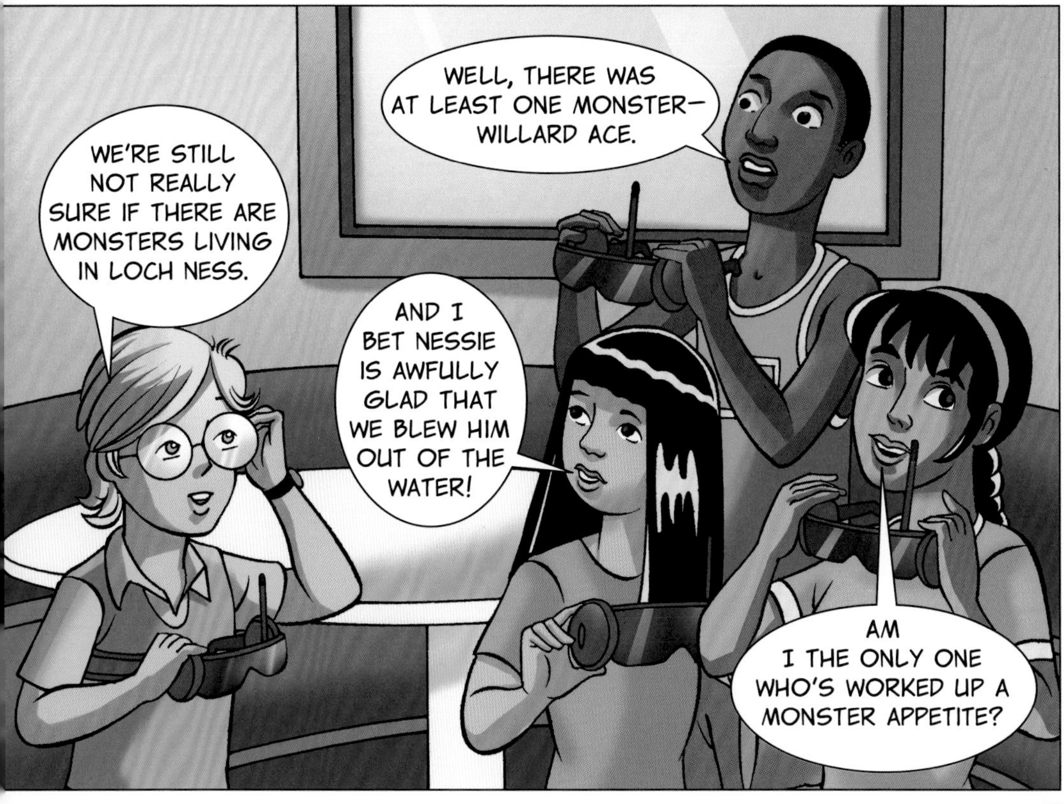
WE'RE STILL NOT REALLY SURE IF THERE ARE MONSTERS LIVING IN LOCH NESS.
WELL, THERE WAS AT LEAST ONE MONSTER—WILLARD ACE.
AND I BET NESSIE IS AWFULLY GLAD THAT WE BLEW HIM OUT OF THE WATER!
AM I THE ONLY ONE WHO'S WORKED UP A MONSTER APPETITE?

FACT FILE

Tectonic: From the Greek *tektonikos* from *tekton* meaning *carpenter*. Having to do with structural changes in the earth's crust.

Plate tectonics: The study of the earth's surface based on the concept of moving plates forming its structure.

Plate: In geology, each of several rigid sheets of rock thought to form the earth's outer crust.

Fault: In geology, an extended break in a strata or vein; a place where tectonic plates push against each other. The Great Glen fault lies under the Scottish Highlands. The San Andreas fault causes earthquakes in California.

FACT FILE

Tartan: A pattern of colored stripes crossing at right angles; the special plaids worn in the Scottish Highlands where each clan had its own pattern. Before the British overturned clan rule, Highlanders wore tartans to proclaim loyalty to their clan.

Horseshoe crab: A large marine arthropod with a horseshoe-shaped shell and a long tail-spine, also called a king crab; an example of an animal that has survived in the same form for over 200 million years!

Eel: Any of various snakelike fish with a slender body and poorly developed fins.

FACT FILE

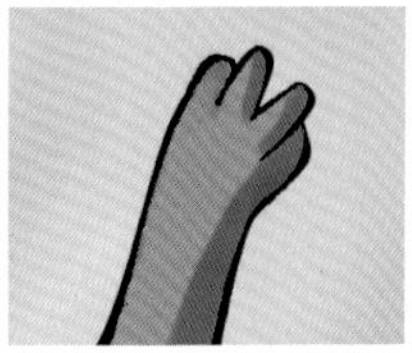

Flipper: A broadened limb of a penguin, seal, plesiosaur, etc., used in swimming. Some Nessie sightings mention flippers, which would account for the creature's ability to swim very fast.

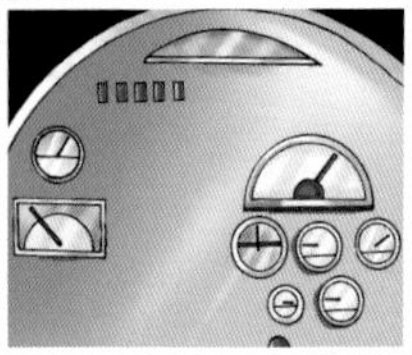

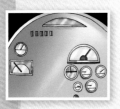

Sonar: A system for the underwater detection of objects using reflected or emitted sound. Radar uses pulses of electromagnetic waves to locate moving planes, ships, or other objects. Sonar works in the same way but using sound waves under water. "Radar" is short for "radio detecting and ranging," while sonar stands for "sound navigation ranging." So far, despite the repeated use of sonar, the Loch Ness monster has not been found!

Find Out for Yourself

Einstein's casebook covered lots of Nessie theories. By researching some of these topics, maybe you can come up with your own:

- Famous Loch Ness monster sightings (starting with the St. Columba story, through the 1715 General Wade's South Road builders; 1933 North Road builders and the rash of sightings that followed; Aldie Mackay and his wife, the surgeon's photo, and more!)
- Sea serpents, giant squids, and other sea monsters
- The use of submarines and sonar to track the Loch Ness monster
- Scotland's large and amazing animals
- How plate tectonics formed the Scottish Highlands

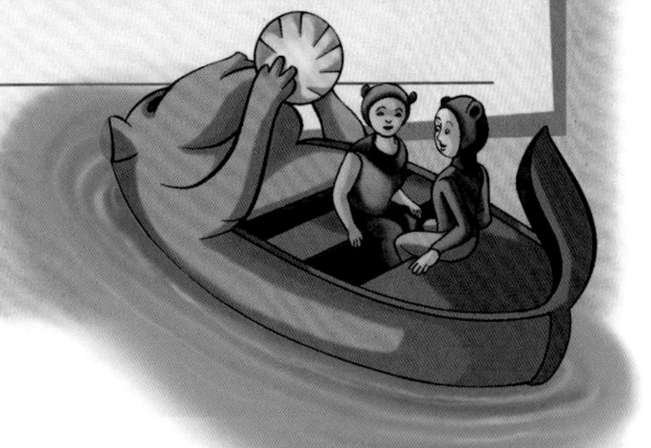

Web Sites

To ensure the currency and safety of recommended Internet links, Windmill maintains and updates an online list of sites related to the subject of this book. To access this list of Web sites, please go to **www.windmillbks.com/weblinks** and select this book's title.

About the Author/Artist

Justine and Ron Fontes met at a publishing house in New York City, where he worked for the comic book department and she was an editorial assistant in children's books. Together, they have written over 500 children's books, in every format from board books to historical novels. They live in Maine, where they continue their work in writing and comics and publish a newsletter, *critter news*.

For more great fiction and nonfiction, go to www.windmillbooks.com